# Wider Horizons

# Wider Horizons

by

## Dorothy Martin

**MOODY PRESS**
CHICAGO

© 1964, 1985 by
THE MOODY BIBLE INSTITUTE
OF CHICAGO
**Revised Edition**

Original title: *Wider Horizons for Peggy*

Scripture quotations
are from the *New King James Version*.

ISBN: 0-8024-8307-0

1 2 3 4 5 6 7 Printing/LC/Year 90 89 88 87 86 85

*Printed in the United States of America*

# 1

**P**eggy lost track of the number of times she had looked at her watch that afternoon. Each time she was sure it must have stopped because time couldn't *possibly* go by that slowly when a person was busy.

She felt the trickle of perspiration on her forehead and wiped it off with the back of her hand, hating the thought of how awful she must look with her limp hair plastered around the back of her neck. *I must look terrible*, she thought, not comforted by seeing that everyone else looked the same way.

It was the fifth straight day of a stifling heat wave that had wilted personalities and frazzled nerves and made everyone edgy. Peggy had to make herself smile at the customers even though she couldn't stand the sight of them. She wondered crossly why they couldn't stay home during this hot weather instead of piling into the store. There were the petulant shoppers who blamed the clerks when they couldn't find what they were looking for; the absentminded ones who bought more than they could pay for, and then she had to fool around making out a return slip; and the customers who tried to exchange items and got angry when they had to talk to the manager. And then there were the children, the constant stream of children, buying suckers and gum and cheap toys and trying to dart into line in front of other shoppers.

She hated to work the cash register anyway because she was still so afraid of making a mistake. Even being stuck in the hot basement stock room counting innumerable boxes of things was better than being out in the public eye like this. She knew she ought to be grateful even to have a job, after spending almost the whole summer looking for one. She had started hunting before school was out last spring and had left her name at practically every store in town and even at the library. She thought longingly now of how nice and quiet the library would be. Books didn't yak at you all the time the way people did.

As she rang up purchases almost automatically, an angry voice said loudly, "Just a minute, young lady! I gave you a ten-dollar bill."

Peggy looked uncertainly at the change for a five the woman was holding in her hand and then down at the bill, which should be lying on the edge of the cash register and wasn't. She was sure the woman had given her a five. But now she couldn't prove it since there were stacks of both fives and tens in the separate compartments of the cash register.

The woman went on in loud tones. "You girls stand here daydreaming when you should be paying attention to your job. Now I want the correct change for my ten dollars."

Peggy bit her lip and looked helplessly at the man standing next in line. "It—it really was a five, wasn't it?" she pleaded.

He looked away from the appeal in her eyes and voice and fumbled with a package he held. "I—uh, I didn't notice. Wasn't close enough. If she said it was a ten, it must have been a ten."

The manager had come over by then, and the woman made her strident complaints to him. Peggy listened miserably, wishing she could drop through the floor, wishing she had never got the job in the first place, wishing she were anywhere but right there.

"Just give her change for a ten," the manager said quietly and watched while she counted it out with shaking voice and fumbling fingers. She was so conscious of the watchful eyes of everyone else in the line, and of the manager's close attention, that she could hardly count correctly.

He stood beside her while she checked out the other four shoppers. Then when there was a break in the line, he said, "You know why that happened, don't you?"

She nodded, angry at herself for her stupid mistake and angry at the woman.

"Always remember to leave the money in plain sight on the ledge of the register until you've returned the change and the customer has accepted it and gone on. Then, if there's any doubt on your part or question on theirs about it, you have your proof."

Peggy nodded. "I'm sorry. I usually do that, but this time I forgot."

"Almost everyone does at some time or other when they first start out." He smiled at her reassuringly.

Peggy was so relieved that he wasn't going to bawl her out or fire her that she said fervently, "I'll never forget again. But I'm still positive she only gave me a five."

"You'll know when you check your drawer tonight. If you're short, you'll know she cheated you." He started away and then stopped and turned. "By the way, if you are short, remember I told you that I'll have to take the difference out of your check this week. That helps make sure you don't make the same mistake twice."

Peggy nodded, knowing she couldn't afford many mistakes like that. Telling about it at dinner

7

that evening, she said, "I was positive I was right at the time, but I guess they always have to believe the customer. By the time they totaled my register at closing time and found I was short, it was too late to do anything about it."

"You'll have to nail her for it the next time she comes in the store," Bill suggested, but Peggy shook her head.

"I don't think I'd know her again. I was so busy trying to figure out the money deal that I hardly looked at her. I'd know the man again, though. It's funny," she went on thoughtfully. "I'm sure he knew I was right, but he just didn't say so."

"He didn't want to get mixed up in something that wasn't any of his business," Mrs. Andrews said tartly. "You can't blame him for that. People are like that more and more these days."

"It wasn't only that," Peggy said. "It was as though he knew he *should* speak up but—" she shrugged. "Oh, well, no use hashing it over now. The money's gone, and that's that."

"There are a lot of people like that," her father said into the silence. "Afraid to take a stand on an issue because it might cause them personal inconvenience or involve them in something unpleasant."

"There's never anything wrong in minding your own business," his wife insisted sharply, a frown etching her forehead in familiar lines of annoyance.

"Yeah, but it sure would have helped Peggy out if that guy had spoken up." Bill began to argue, but Peggy stopped him with a tired gesture.

"It was my fault anyway, really. I'd had it drummed into me to leave the money out in plain sight, and I forgot. As long as it doesn't happen again, I guess I can stand to lose a few dollars."

She wanted to change the subject because she sensed another of the endless differences building

8

between her parents. She felt too dragged out to be involved in any discussion that meant thinking through an issue and taking sides. Their family had had too many such issues through the years, personal problems that had threatened to tear the family apart. She knew the problems were fewer since her father had been saved, because he tried to be more patient and understanding. But with her mother always so critical and edgy, explosions still flared up unexpectedly.

"I'll be glad when some of the kids get back from vacation," she said quickly before Bill could go on with the argument. He had such a one-track mind when something like this got started.

"It has been kind of dead the last few weeks," Bill agreed. "I'm waiting for Jim to get back. It's rough doing all the lawns by myself. It didn't seem like so many when we split the work."

"Yeah, but remember you also had to split the money. And, anyway, think what it's doing for those muscles you keep talking about."

"How about some tennis tonight?" Bill asked, ignoring her last remark.

Peggy shook her head. "I'm beat, and it's still too hot. How come you didn't ask Candy?"

"I did, and she can't. Her mother's got some fancy thing on, and she's supposed to help."

"Oh." She didn't have to ask what the fancy thing would be like. She had stopped at Candy's house once when her mother had a party going, and the air had been heavy with smoke and the room loud with the laughter of people who had had too much to drink. Candy was like her mother in appearance—slim and vivacious with a cap of shining black hair. But there the resemblance ended. Candy was sweet and affectionate and warmly friendly, while her mother was —Peggy searched for a word while she absentmindedly surveyed Bill's lanky figure stretched out on the sofa.

9

"Brittle," she said and didn't realize she had said it out loud until Bill looked at her, startled, and said, "Huh?"

"I was thinking of Candy's mother."

"She's wacky!" he exclaimed. "She doesn't like me too much."

"That's because she thinks you're a bad influence on her darling daughter. You drag her to too many church things. Not that she needs any dragging," she added in response to Bill's protest. "But don't forget you *are* responsible for her coming to our church," she reminded him slyly, remembering Candy's frank, open admission of how she had found the church.

"Aw, cut it out," he retorted and jumped up when the phone rang.

"Yes, sir," Peggy heard him answer and thought it must be an adult on the other end to make him sound so polite.

"Well, I don't know," she heard him say. "I can find out. I'm sure I can come, but I don't know about Peggy. I'll find out and call you back. How long will you be in town? . . . OK. And thanks. Thanks a lot."

"What was that all about?"

"Mr. Parker. He had to come in for a funeral and wants to know if we want to go back with him to the lake tomorrow for over Sunday. This is the last weekend of their vacation."

"What time is he going?"

"He didn't say. The funeral is in the afternoon."

"If he can wait until after five-thirty, I can make it." She gave a long sigh. "I don't care that I'm not much good at swimming. I just want to sit in that cool lake water. It will be wonderful to get out of this heat."

"When will he bring you back?" Her mother's practical question jolted her out of her dreamy anticipation, and she looked at Bill.

"I didn't think to ask him. He invited us for the weekend—no, over Sunday was what he actually said. But Jim told me before they went that they wouldn't be back until Wednesday."

"And I'd have to be here Monday morning by the time the store opens at nine." Peggy sighed again, this time with disappointment. "I guess it won't work out after all."

When Bill called Mr. Parker back, he urged her to come. "I'll see that you get back in time for work Monday."

But Peggy knew it would mean a seventy-five-mile round trip for him and decided that was asking too much of him, even though he was willing to do it.

"Anyway, I'd probably stay up late Sunday night talking to Ann and make more mistakes than ever at work," she said as she helped her mother clean up the kitchen Saturday evening.

Her mother made some answer, but Peggy's mind had gone off in another direction, wondering if Larry was back yet. He had gone to California right after graduation and, through his uncle, had got a job in one of the state parks about fifty miles from where Lisa lived.

She remembered Ann's saying, "They're both so sure of the future it's almost scary. Lots of kids right out of high school don't even know what college they want to go to. But Larry and Lisa have their whole lives mapped out."

"Are they going to finish college before they get married?" As she asked, the memory of that bitter afternoon when her dreams about Larry had crashed in a heap stirred in her mind, and she was glad the memory no longer hurt so sharply.

"Yes. Then Larry is going to seminary and have a part-time job, and Lisa will work, too."

"It must be wonderful to have everything planned out so perfectly." Peggy knew her voice

11

sounded wistful and hurried to cover it by asking, "But I thought Lisa was planning to come here and go to the university where Larry is going."

"Larry suggested that, but Lisa wouldn't do it. She has a scholarship to a college near her home, and she couldn't afford to pass that up. And anyway, she said she couldn't leave home yet. She said there was too much unfinished business there. Her dad, I suppose she means. He still doesn't do anything to help support the family."

*Unfinished business.* The words echoed now in Peggy's mind as she followed her mother out to the porch where her father sat on the swing in the soft dusk.

She perched on the porch railing, grateful for the slight breeze that gently lifted the leaves of the trees and rustled the shrubs that sprawled along the length of the porch. The remembered conversation with Ann had started a trail of memories. She thought of the many times she had sat on the porch like this, swinging from one mood to another, sometimes way up, sometimes way down, depending on what problem she was facing. Thinking back now, she had to admit that even though some of the problems had loomed like mountains, they had always smoothed out. In fact, most of them now were only a blur in her memory, and that was annoying when she remembered all the time she had wasted worrying about them. The worrying hadn't helped solve them. The trouble was, it was hard to remember that when she most needed to.

Her mind cautiously skirted the two problems that she thought about every day, because she prayed about them in her devotions each morning. The most important was her mother's salvation, which seemed as remote a possibility as it had four years ago when she herself had become a Christian. Her mother refused to listen, and all they could do was pray for her to find in Christ the peace and joy she so desperately needed.

Peggy thought of how much she had prayed for that since that cold December day when Larry and Lisa had so unwittingly closed her out of their world. She had had a glimpse that day of the emptiness in her mother's life, and she had not been able to forget it.

She shifted to sit down on the porch and brace her back against the post, feeling restless. Thinking of that day only opened the longing of her other prayer, which still hadn't been answered. She could now think of Larry without a quiver, but that didn't take away her wish that *someone* would think her special.

She had mentioned the subject once, carefully, to Mrs. Springer, who said in her usual forthright way, "My goodness, Peggy, do you think God keeps us from having what we want if it's best for us to have it?"

Then, not giving her a chance to answer, she had gone on briskly, "We forget that God can see what we can't. We only see the now, but God knows the end from the beginning. One girl I went to school with gave her boyfriend her picture for a Christmas present and signed it, 'Forever yours.' Two days later she was going steady with someone else. We're *so* shortsighted. We can be thankful God isn't and that He keeps us from our own foolish mistakes. Don't rush things, Peggy. Wait for the right person."

"But—what if—what if that never happens?" Peggy asked, not prepared for the sober look on Mrs. Springer's face or for the unexpected answer.

"Then that will be God's will for you."

"But I don't want that!" she blurted, not caring how it sounded.

Mrs. Springer nodded. "I know how hard it is to think this through, and I can't give you easy help.

But I can remind you of a verse you already know. Remember the first two verses of Romans twelve? They talk about God's will, but what they really emphasize is that we have to accept God's will *first*, and then we'll know that we want it."

She reached a comforting arm around Peggy. "Sometimes I'm a little amused at the tragic faces of sixteen-year-olds who think life has passed them by. Just enjoy life, and wait for the Lord to do what you think is impossible."

Peggy tried to follow her advice and not let herself wish for dates. It helped having Ellen to go around with, because she seemed indifferent to dating. But sometimes it was hard always being either the third person in the car with Ann and Bob or Alice and Dan or else lumped in with a bunch of girls.

*Like tonight for instance,* she thought moodily. Of course she liked her parents, but there was a limit to the amount of time a person wanted to spend sitting around with them. Even school was better than this because at least *something* was going on. Maybe when everyone got back from vacation they could plan something big to start off the year.

# 2

The shrill ring of the phone cut across the stillness of the night, and Peggy jumped. "I'll get it," she said and realized how unnecessary the remark was since neither of her parents had moved. But the automatic hope that sprang into her mind flickered and died when she answered and heard Candy say, "Hi."

She bit back a mean impulse to say, "Sorry, Bill's not here." But Candy seldom phoned him and probably knew that he had gone to the Parkers' for the weekend.

"I just got a brainstorm," Candy bubbled. "Why don't we throw a party for all the kids who are going away to school? We could really make a big thing of it."

"Good idea! I was sitting here sort of thinking of that myself."

"And at the same time we could try to get in a bunch of new kids. It's going to leave kind of a big hole when everyone goes who's going. If we have a really super party, we could invite all kinds of kids."

"When would we have it? And where? Are you thinking of an indoor thing or a cookout or something?"

"I haven't thought that far yet. It'll depend on the weather and stuff like that. Do you think we can work out something neat?" Candy's voice was eager and warm and poured out, Peggy thought, like rich cream.

"Sure, why not? Only we should talk it over with the Springers."

"I already have, and they're all for it."

"We'll have to have it real soon," Peggy warned. "Ann and Bob leave in about ten days, and probably Larry and the others about the same time."

"Let's get at it right away. We can get ideas lined up even if we don't know the date for sure."

"Why don't we just decide right now to have an outdoor hamburger bash? I think everyone would go for that. Then if it rains we'll just have to change at the last minute. I'll find out when the college kids are leaving and let you know," Peggy promised.

Candy put her usual zip into the plans and called a few days later with a list of people she thought should be invited. Some of the names Peggy didn't know at all, and others she frowned over. She was being unreasonable, she knew, but their group was perfect as it was without getting in a lot of kids who would be alien in their outlook.

"We do want this to be a special good-bye for the ones who've been in the group all this time," she reminded Candy, trying to choose her words carefully and not put a damper on the whole idea.

"That's just it," Candy replied enthusiastically. "When these new people see what a great bunch we have, it's sure to get them interested. Of course they still have to be invited."

"Do you know them all?"

"Oh, no! I don't have any idea who some of them are. A couple of us went through the yearbook, and everyone picked out names they knew or knew about. They're all mixed up—seniors and juniors and some freshmen. Sophomores, too, of course."

"Well, I guess what I'm really wondering is, are they the kind who would be interested in coming to our meetings?"

16

"N-no, not all of them. But they all need it," Candy answered simply, and Peggy felt rebuked even though she was sure Candy didn't mean to sound unkind. One thing about her—she was direct, like Ellen. You always knew where you stood with her.

"But what I called you about," Candy was going on, "was to find out how you think we should invite them. Do we see them personally, or call them, or what? And should there be a committee to do it, or maybe the seniors should invite the seniors and so on. What do you think?"

After hashing it over and talking to Mrs. Springer, they decided to invite the new people personally.

"And listen, let's double invite them," Candy said. "Let's have a guy and a girl invite each one. A girl might turn down a girl who asked her, but she wouldn't refuse an invitation from a guy."

"And it will work the other way, too," Peggy agreed.

But she frowned over the four names assigned to her, positive her effort would be wasted. Two of the names were girls who had been in history with her last year and who were only mildly interested in the party. The third was a freshman who had just moved into the school district and was pathetically eager to get invited to anything. The fourth, Phyllis, was the one she dreaded asking, and she put off doing it.

"I don't know her at all," she complained to Ellen. "But you've seen her in the halls at school, haven't you?" She knew Ellen had. You only had to look at her heavy mascara with the black eyeliner and the smudges of green eye shadow to know that church was the last thing Phyllis was interested in. "And isn't she the one who dyed her hair purple last year? Or was it green?"

17

Ellen nodded. "Green, I think. You know, Peggy, she doesn't do much talking, but she's always the center of that loud gang that hangs around after school. They never sit on the bleachers at games even though they always come. I'm glad you've got her to ask, and not me."

Peggy put off calling Phyllis, not knowing what to say. She couldn't just barge in and say, "Pardon me, but would you like to come to a church party?" She could just bet what kind of an answer that would get. Every time she thought seriously about phoning, it was too late in the evening or something else came up, and so she let it slide. She did have a twinge of guilt when she saw Phyllis in the store one day buying fingernail polish. When she saw the wild colors Phyllis picked out, it confirmed her certainty that Phyllis would laugh at the invitation. And anyway, Candy had said she was going to give her name to one of the guys to ask her. That would be the only kind of invitation Phyllis would listen to.

They planned the party for the second weekend in September since most of the college kids were leaving early the next week. By that Saturday the heat wave broke, and the day was just hot enough to feel good if you were outside where there was a breeze. In the store Peggy was hot since the air-conditioning still wasn't working right, and she could hardly wait for closing time.

Most of the group had gone out to the picnic grounds early in the afternoon. But Ellen had offered to come back and get her at six, which would just give her time to get home and change and be ready in time. When she came out of the store, she heard a car horn blare and saw Ellen parked at the curb.

"I thought I'd pick you up and run you home. That will save you some time, and we'll be sure to make it in time to eat."

18

"Thanks, Ellen. I'll do something nice for you someday." Peggy slid into the car and exclaimed, "Ouch!" as she touched the plastic seat covers.

"I know. I didn't have sense enough to park under a tree this afternoon," Ellen sympathized. "But I'm glad my mother let me have the car, at least. I think she's still surprised that I passed my driver's test the first time." She looked carefully before pulling out into traffic and then asked, "You're not going to work after school starts, are you?"

"Some. The manager said I could work every Saturday and during vacations if I want to. The catch is that I have to agree to work after school or evenings when the store is open if they need me. Like if someone gets sick or doesn't show up. I said I would because I can sure use the money. My closet is bare, and I don't have time to sew anything."

Then, as Ellen pulled into the driveway, she said, "It won't take me long to change. Come on in."

"OK. It'll be cooler in than out, and I can sure use a cold drink of water."

Peggy caught the screen door behind them and called, "Hi," in the general direction of the kitchen. "Sit down, and I'll get us something cold to drink. My mother believes in lemonade. Is that OK?"

"It's not my favorite, but I'll settle for it if it's cold."

Her mother looked up from the cake she was frosting. "I hope Bill left some lemonade. He brought four or five others in with him this afternoon, and they acted as though they had been a month on the desert."

Peggy burst out laughing. "I'll bet he succeeded in that Tom Sawyer thing he planned. Did he say anything about it?"

"What do you mean?"

Peggy turned to Ellen, who had followed her to the kitchen and stood leaning against the doorframe. "He had these three really big lawns to mow this morning, and he didn't think he'd get done in time. So he was going to con a couple of guys into helping by letting them 'have the fun' of trying out his new mower. Knowing Bill, it probably worked."

Peggy laughed again as she filled the glasses and turned to go into the living room. Her mother called after her, "By the way, a phone call came for Bill just after he left. Some girl calling about your party tonight."

"Candy?" Peggy asked and then answered herself. "Couldn't have been. She and Bill were going out early."

"No, she's been there all afternoon. She's got a long list of stuff, and she checks off when everyone shows up with what they're supposed to bring or do. She's Miss Efficiency herself. In a nice way," Ellen added quickly.

"Did she say who she was?" Peggy called back to her mother.

"No. Or, at least I don't think she did. There was so much racket going on in the background, I could hardly hear a word she said. One of those loud—what do you call them?—was blaring out. They used to call them jukeboxes in my day. I don't see why they allow those things in public places. The noise only aggravates most people."

Peggy only half-listened to her mother's complaints as she puzzled over who the person was. She had seen Candy's list and knew that all those who said they were coming had a way.

"I hope someone hasn't been overlooked," Ellen said. "If we knew who it was, she could ride with us. It would be too bad for someone to miss out when we're right here."

"Oh, well." Peggy shrugged. "There's nothing we can do about it. Anyway, I've rushed so much today, I don't want to think any more than I have to. Sit down, Ellen. I'll be ready in a couple of minutes."

# 3

A quick shower and a change into a shirt and cutoffs made her feel better, and she was really looking forward to the evening by the time Ellen pulled into the parking lot of the picnic grounds.

"Looks like a lot of people are having picnics," Peggy said, looking around at all the cars.

"I think Candy said that we got the last big place that has a shelter in case it rains. It looks like most of the others are just bunches of families having picnic suppers."

They walked to the picnic area and found Mrs. Springer spreading out stacks of food on the long tables the boys had shoved together.

"Where's the committee that's supposed to be doing all this?" Peggy looked around as she asked, feeling a little angry. That committee had it a lot easier than the one *she'd* been on, and it wasn't fair for them to weasel out.

But Mrs. Springer laughed. "Oh, I sent them off, including my husband. They were crazy to get in on the games. I've had my day at blowing up balloons, and running relays and three-legged races, and trying to stuff down dry crackers just to win a useless prize. This is my speed right here. In fact, they're playing some crazy game over there now that's new since my time."

"I hope Bill brought our stuff," Peggy said, stopping to sample a pickle. "I don't suppose he'd forget though, since it was food."

"Even the cake got here whole." Mrs. Springer smiled at her in return. She looked around at Ellen, who had spotted a basketball hoop and a loose ball, and turned to Peggy with a laugh. "You know, I've finally found someone my boys are crazy about. I know they're only eight, but I had just about decided that I would still have them underfoot when they were fifty because they have such an aversion to girls. But they like Ellen because she plays their type of games, which most baby-sitters don't want to do. She's the only one they're willing to have stay with them when we go out. It's funny, too," she said, her voice serious, "because with those pretty curls and nice figure, she isn't a bit like a boy."

"She's just a natural athlete," Peggy agreed as she watched Ellen sink a basket. "If some college coach knew what he was missing just because she's a girl, he'd be sick." She laughed and stood up. "If you really don't need help, I'll wander over and see what everyone is doing. I don't think I'm up to any games myself. I'm hungry, but not enough to eat dry crackers." She smiled at Mrs. Springer and waited while Ellen threw a final basket.

"Let everyone know we'll be eating in about fifteen minutes," Mrs. Springer called after them.

"When I got here earlier and saw the food, I thought the food committee had gone off its rocker. I didn't think we'd ever eat all the stuff, not even with Bill here. But a lot of other kids have come since I went back for you. Looks like fifty or sixty ganged up over there."

"Yeah, and quite a lot of them look new." Peggy shaded her eyes from the sun as she looked around. "You've really got to hand it to Candy. When she gets an idea, she goes all out on it. Of course, she had committees helping, but she was the one who really worked up enthusiasm for the party."

22

"Hi!" Ann collapsed on the grass beside them with a groan. "I can't take it any longer. Someone take my place, please."

Ellen charged into the volleyball game, leaping to spike a ball. But Peggy dropped onto the grass beside Ann. "I'm beat. My feet keep telling me to get off them." She looked around. "Where did all these kids come from?"

"I don't know, but it's wonderful to have so many. Let's hope they all turn out for the meeting tomorrow."

"That's the whole idea behind this party. We've got to get in a mob to take the place of you kids who are leaving."

"Not a mob," Ann protested. "There aren't that many of us leaving. Just Larry and Bob and Joyce—"

"And you and Marian and Betty, and I think Steve. Seven, at least," Peggy counted. "And some of you are worth ten of the rest of us," she added. She looked out across the field where some of the guys were yelling their way through a soccer game.

"Take Bob, for instance," she said and then laughed as Ann, her eyes crinkling in an answering laugh, said, "Thanks, I will."

"Things are really going to be dead at first with all of you gone," Peggy insisted. "I hope we don't fold."

"How could you?" Ann asked. "Think of all who're left—you and Bill and Candy and Ellen and Jim. Too many to name."

"Who can take your place at the piano?"

"Lois."

Peggy stared at her. "Lois? She never says two words to anyone. Besides, I didn't know she played. How do you know she does?"

"I heard her once when she thought nobody was around. She's so bashful she didn't want anyone to

23

know. I got Alice to work on her and build up her self-confidence. After all, Alice could understand how she felt better than any of the rest of us. We decided to keep it a secret until the last meeting before I leave. You'll all have to encourage her, though, because she's really scared."

Peggy listened, wondering what else went on with people in the group that she didn't know anything about. And she felt ashamed that she had been so insensitive about Lois, seeing only her bashfulness and feeling impatient with her because of it.

She saw Ann gesture at the figures milling around in the field, and her voice was thoughtful as she said, "There's no telling who the Lord has in that bunch that He's planning to use this year."

A piercing whistle from the direction of the tables arrested everyone in mid-action momentarily, making them look like still pictures. Then there was a rush as eveyone tried to be first in line.

"When are you going?" Peggy asked, waiting with Ann until Bob caught up with them.

"Monday, early. I'm riding with Bob, of course, but my parents are driving also because Bob doesn't have room in his car for his stuff and mine. Anyway, my mother wanted to see if any of her classmates are bringing their children to school. She's more excited about it than I am."

"Come on, let's get in line before all the food is gone," Peggy urged. But Ann had turned and was staring off toward the parking lot. Peggy turned, too, and saw three figures sauntering across the grass toward them. One was a girl in skintight black pants and a bulky purple sweater, the sleeves pushed up to her elbows. Phyllis with the two guys she usually hung around with. *Or who usually hang around her*, Peggy corrected herself. They stopped a little distance away from the grills where the hamburgers and hot dogs were broiling and returned the stares of the group. Peggy couldn't help thinking that they were like two opposing camps, the good guys and the bad guys.

Then Alice broke the strained silence with a bright, and to Peggy's ears insincere-sounding, "Hi, you guys. Glad you decided to come."

And Bob echoed quickly, "You're just in time for the food. Shove in line here. You can meet everyone while we're eating."

Phyllis's eyes flickered first toward Alice and then toward Bob. There was a moment of warmth in them which faded as she surveyed the rest of the group. Then she saw Bill, and once again Peggy saw a flare of emotion until her eyes moved to take in Candy who stood some distance from Bill, the expression on her face welcoming but guarded.

The Springers finally broke the tableau, urging everyone to get started unless they wanted the ants to have it, and the line began to move. Peggy looked around and saw the newcomers at the end of the line with Bob and Bill. If those two weren't successful in making them feel welcome, nobody would be.

*.But whatever made them come?* she wondered, and found her thoughts repeated by Ellen, standing in front of her, who half-turned her head to mutter, "Who invited those characters?"

"The thing I'm wondering is *why* they came," she replied. "They look as though they would just love to break up the party." She balanced her loaded plate and a can of soda and found a place at one of the tables. "You want to save a place with us for Bob?"

Ann nodded. "And save some extra places."

Ellen looked around. "Is Candy eating with us?"

Ann shook her head quickly. "No, she's staying to help Mrs. Springer." She flashed a quick smile as Bob stopped by the table.

"I hope you're saving these places for us. You girls know Phyllis. And this is Roy and Mike."

The newcomers stared, their faces expressionless, and then sat down. Peggy couldn't help noticing the provocative fragrance of the expensive perfume that drifted in her direction. Bill was on the other side of Phyllis next to Roy. He didn't seem to have any trouble finding something to talk about, though Peggy hid a laugh as she saw Roy eating steadily, not bothering to answer.

Something Bill said brought a response to Phyllis's expressionless gray eyes, and she turned to look at Peggy with unexpected interest.

"You two are related?" she asked, her surprise clear.

Peggy nodded and stared back with what she intended to be a cold look. She wondered if it was the color or the amount of eye shadow that Phyllis wore that gave her eyes such an odd appearance. There was something strange about the way she looked at a person. Peggy felt as though she were looking down a long corridor where there was no light, and it made her shiver involuntarily.

Then she told herself she was being silly. After one long stare, Phyllis turned away and didn't look in Peggy's direction again. But she did seem awfully interested in Alice and kept looking down the length of the table to where she sat with Dan and a bunch of other kids. Candy finally sat down there, too. Peggy could see that her usually vivid, expressive face wore a strained, anxious look.

Bob and Bill gave all their attention to Roy and Mike and went back with them repeatedly for more food. Between them they kept up a steady flow of conversation on various subjects. They didn't let the fact that they didn't get much response bother them, Peggy noticed. She envied, as she had so often, Bill's gift of getting along with people. Here she was, sitting like a dumb cluck, not having the faintest idea what to say to Phyllis. Even if Phyllis turned in her direction, she wouldn't know how to get a conversation going.

She wondered what strategy the boys would use to spark some interest when it was time to get serious after supper. Somehow they managed to keep the three of them surrounded by the regulars of the church group. If the visitors had planned to cause trouble, they didn't have a chance to carry it out during the neat program the committee had planned.

The group singing was brief, and Peggy assumed that was because a lot of the new kids wouldn't know the choruses they usually sang. Bill and Jim had brought their instruments, which helped keep the singing lively. They also played a duet, and Peggy, sitting where she could see Phyllis, was bothered by her intent expression as she watched Bill and listened. She glanced over at Candy and saw her watching Phyllis, an oddly troubled look on her face.

The Springers were introduced as the new adult sponsors of the group. Wild applause and cries of, "Speech! Speech!" were followed by fake groans as Mr. Springer stood up. "I thought you'd never ask," he said, and pulled a thick pad of papers from his pocket.

He started out in his usual low-key way. "I had a man come to see me the other day, wanting to sell me some life insurance. You know what he talked about first? Death. That's a logical place for a life insurance man to start, isn't it? After all, if we're going to live forever, we don't need life insurance. But that fellow knows I won't, and he wanted to get me ready to die. Now, of course, when I take out life insurance it won't keep me from dying. It just helps me know that my family will be taken care of.

27

"The Bible talks about death, too, though a different kind. In fact, by the Bible's definition we can be dead even while we're alive. Every time we do something wrong we show that we are dying. That's what sin brings—death.

"But God offers life in place of death. Eternal life. It's a gift that can't be earned or deserved. It's free."

He stopped in the quietness to look around at the listening group. "Maybe some of you haven't thought much about God. Maybe some of you don't believe He exists." He shook his head. "That doesn't change the fact that He is God. And He is the only one who can give life in place of death. I don't know a better insurance policy than that."

Bob stood up. "Before we wind this up, I'd just like to say something to anyone who is hearing all this for the first time. If it sounds unbelievable, it is—until you believe it. A couple of years ago you couldn't have convinced me that there even was a God. But I know what Jesus Christ can do. All I can do is tell you what He has done for me."

Peggy had sat listening—critically, she feared—wondering what Phyllis was thinking. Had any of this made an impression on her or on any of the others there for the first time? She was aware that the party was breaking up and got up to help gather the trash. Ellen volunteered her car to take back some of the equipment they had borrowed from the church. Peggy climbed into the car to wait, tiredness catching up with her, while Ellen looked around for anyone who needed a ride.

She came back alone just as Bob slammed the trunk and came around to lean his arm on the edge of the open window. "If you come ten minutes early to Sunday school tomorrow, I'll unload that stuff." Then he smiled at them. "Wasn't this an unexpected bonus to have those three show up? Bill didn't know what good results he would have with that one invitation. He not only got Phyllis but Roy and Mike, too. Of course, maybe it wasn't his invitation alone. You know Candy had it planned so that two people invited each person. Now the thing to do is keep them coming until a spark of interest catches hold and they find out what it's all about."

"It won't ever happen to them."

Bob looked at her in surprise. "Why not?"

Not noticing the tone of his voice, she answered crossly, "You can tell by looking at them that they're not the type to be saved."

He straightened up and looked down at her. Then he said, "I didn't know there was *anyone* who couldn't be a Christian. I was their 'type' myself not too long ago. That's why I said what I did." He turned and stalked off without a backward look.

Peggy and Ellen stared after him wordlessly, until Ellen gave a low whistle. "Boy! I guess we've been told!"

# 4

Peggy wakened sometime during the night, wondering vaguely what time it was, conscious that she didn't feel well. She couldn't focus her eyes on the clock's lighted dial and tossed restlessly, sleeping only fitfully. Hearing her mother start downstairs to get breakfast, she managed to call loudly enough to be heard. When Mrs. Andrews saw her flushed face and the feverish look in her eyes, she went for the thermometer.

"Yes, it's well over a hundred. No getting up for you today."

"I suppose I'd better stay in bed," Peggy agreed, feeling too miserable to argue. "I can't imagine what's wrong. I felt fine yesterday, except for being kind of tired."

"It's probably due to a mixture of too many pickles and salad, and cake, with cold drinks gulped too fast," her mother said unsympathetically.

"If that's the reason, then Bill should be the one to be sick," Peggy answered feebly, pulling the covers up gratefully to drift into an uneasy sleep. She slept most of the day, not caring what went on around her, yet somehow conscious of sounds in the house. She was dimly aware that she would miss a final get-together after church before the college crowd left, but couldn't fight her way up enough to regret not being there.

Bill looked into her room in the late afternoon, his trumpet case banging against the door as he tried to be quiet. "Sorry you can't make it," he whispered loudly and waited for her answer. She lay still, the effort to frame an intelligent answer too great, and after a moment she heard him leave.

When she opened her eyes again, the sun was shining in through the partially open louvered blinds. She frowned as she looked at the window, wondering what time it was. Finally she realized that it was morning, that she had slept soundly through the night, and that she was ravenous. She got up, glanced at the clock, which said six-thirty, and went downstairs, pulling on a robe. Expecting to find her mother in the kitchen, she stopped abruptly when she saw Bill breaking eggs into a bowl.

He looked around at her. "Hi. You look better, but still kind of beat."

"That's nothing compared to the way Mother will look when she sees this kitchen! How can you make such a mess just fixing a little dab of breakfast?"

"As long as you don't have to clean it up, don't worry about it," he retorted. "I'll take care of it before Mom comes down."

"You don't have all day, you know," she reminded him and put away cereal boxes and stacked dirty dishes in the sink. "I don't see how you can eat so much anyway. First cereal, and then eggs and bacon. Ugh!"

"Want some scrambled eggs?" Bill invited in reply.

She started to refuse, took a second, surprised look at the fluffy mound he held out invitingly, and said, "Sure. I'm so hungry I'll even eat your cooking."

She dropped a slice of bread in the toaster, poured a glass of milk, and asked, "What's your rush today?"

"Got six lawns to mow before noon."

"Why before noon?"

"The afternoon is all sewed up. Tennis first and swimming later on. This is the last day the pool is open."

"Were there a lot of kids at the meeting last night?"

"Yeah, quite a gang. Not as many as were at the picnic, though. Some of the new ones came—mostly girls."

"How about Phyllis and those two guys?" As Peggy asked, she could still hear the quiet rebuke in Bob's voice on Saturday.

"No, they didn't show. I thought sure they would, especially Phyllis, and I guess where she goes, the guys pretty much go. I don't know if you could see her while Mr. Springer and Bob were talking Saturday, but she really looked impressed. Candy called her yesterday to remind her about the meeting. She said she'd think about coming, but she didn't."

Peggy reached into the refrigerator for a jar of preserves saying, "Bob said you were the one who invited her to the cookout." She was glad Bill couldn't read her guilty mind when he answered, "I wasn't supposed to, but whoever had her on his list didn't follow through. So Candy asked me to call her sort of at the last minute."

"How come Candy knows her so well?"

"Their mothers belong to the same club."

"*Their* mothers belong to the same club?" Peggy echoed. "I wouldn't think they were the same type to belong to the same club. Candy's mother is so sophisticated, and Phyllis doesn't look like the type to have a sophisticated, with-it mother. She looks more—well, I don't know the word I want."

"Have you ever seen Phyllis's mother?"

"No. Have you?"

"No, but she and Candy's mother *are* good friends, so they must be the same type. They like the same things, at least," he finished, his voice disgusted.

"It's funny, then, that Candy and Phyllis are so different," she persisted.

"Why funny? Candy is a Christian and Phyllis isn't," Bill answered.

"But Phyllis is so—so—" The word Ellen had used on Saturday came back to her, and she said it out loud. "Hood-y."

"She is," he agreed calmly.

Peggy propped her elbows on the table and rested her chin in her hands as Bill cleared the table and began to load the dishwasher efficiently. She watched his tall, muscular figure stooping slightly over the sink, and her lips quirked in a faint smile. She remembered how little he had been when they first moved to town and how often then he had been the typical little brother—a nuisance. And now he had grown not only in size but in understanding, and perception, and leadership. Most of all, he had grown spiritually.

*Much more than I have*, was the unwelcome thought that pushed its way into her mind. Jerking back from it, she said, "You'll make some girl happy as an automatic dishwasher," and ducked the water he flicked at her.

For some reason, the memory of Candy's face in an unguarded moment at the cookout floated in front of her, a face unusually grave and troubled. As it did, an impossible thought became a certainty. *So that's why Phyllis came!*

She didn't realize she had said it out loud until Bill, half-turning, said, "Why?"

Seeing her knowing smile, he turned red and muttered, "That's the trouble with you girls. You always have to take things personally."

33

"It's true, though, isn't it? Phyllis came because *you* invited her?" she persisted. When he didn't answer, she asked, "How did you get to know her?"

"I've seen her around."

"Who hasn't?" Peggy retorted derisively. "The trouble is recognizing her each time. I think she's tried every color of the rainbow on her hair."

"She was in a couple of my classes last year," he went on, apparently deciding to give more of an explanation. "I always did think she was a person we ought to work on."

"I'm surprised she'd think you were her type," Peggy said, intending it to be a joke. She was not prepared for Bill's sudden swing around to face her and his angry, "Look! Lay off it, will you?"

"You don't have to get mad about it. I was only fooling," she protested, surprised at how angry he seemed. It wasn't like him to blow up so easily over a joke.

"It's not funny!" he insisted heatedly. "I don't want anyone, her especially, to think I'm interested in her that way."

"Well, OK! But I still bet that's the reason she came."

"So? What difference does it make if it turns out all right? If she keeps coming and gets saved?" he demanded.

"It doesn't always work out that easily." She knew she shouldn't have argued when Bill replied, "It worked for Bob, didn't it?"

His words were a reminder of what Bob himself had said, and Peggy had no answer. Now she wondered uneasily if she were being stubborn about Phyllis only because she really didn't think it would do any good. And, of course, if Phyllis only came because of Bill, that wouldn't last long, since Candy was his girl.

She had to admit that she had a guilty feeling about Phyllis because she was supposed to have invited her, and she hadn't done it.

She watched Bill wipe out the sink and hang up the dishtowels he had used. She couldn't tease him anymore, knowing it was in the matter of witnessing that she failed the most in her Christian life. What was so easy for him to do with a friendly grin made her freeze in a panic. She remembered how hard it had been even to talk to Alice and how she had stammered and couldn't find the right words. And Alice had been her best friend. If she had trouble talking naturally about the Lord to people she knew and liked and who knew and liked her, how could she hope to succeed with someone like Phyllis?

Mr. Parker kept telling them, "Just tell people what God has done for you. That's the best kind of witnessing there is." Every time Peggy heard him say that, she felt inhibited, afraid that there hadn't been any change in her that people could see.

It was a sobering thought, and she shook it off by thinking again of Phyllis. Bill would have no problem getting her interest because he was a boy, and Phyllis's type always responded to a boy. She knew Bill would react furiously to that, but she couldn't help it. It was true. So the simplest solution would be to let him go ahead and to not get mixed up with Phyllis herself.

She frowned as she thought again of Candy. She couldn't really think that Bill was interested in Phyllis. She ought to know Bill better than that and know that he only wanted Phyllis to come to church and hear how to be saved. "Maybe I ought to remind her of that in a roundabout way," she muttered as she went upstairs to dress.

The problem came back to bother her later in the day when Alice called to see when she was going to school to register. "Not that I'm crazy to enter that building again," she added with a deep sigh.

"I'm one of those lucky people who start off the alphabet," Peggy reminded her. "I go at nine to-morrow."

"And I go at two in the afternoon. What about Ellen?"

"Wednesday morning, I think"

"I'll go by myself then, I guess. Too bad you were sick yesterday. You really missed a terrific meeting."

"That's what Bill said. And he said you had a good time after church, too."

"And did he tell you about the new talent we've discovered? Would you believe Lois is almost as good at the piano as Ann! She's awfully nervous about taking Ann's place, afraid kids will be comparing her all the time. I know the feeling!"

"Well, at least Lois's looks won't get in the way. I mean, if it were Phyllis, everyone would look at her wild color combinations instead of listening to what she was playing."

Hearing the silence at the other end of the line, Peggy was ashamed of the sarcasm she could hear echoing in her remark. Then Alice said, "We really ought do something special for Phyllis, though."

"Why for her more than anyone else?" Peggy demanded and wondered why *everyone* was talking about Phyllis.

"Oh—I don't know." Peggy could almost see the little, helpless shrug that Alice gave when words failed her.

"Do you know her?"

"Sort of."

Peggy tried to control her impatience, knowing if she gave Alice enough time the explanation would eventually come out in a rush of breathless words.

It did now, as Alice said, "This is just between us, Peggy, but I sort of feel an obligation to her. I know she doesn't look as though she'd ever be interested in anything connected with church. But, you see, she wasn't always this way."

Alice's voice slowed and then stopped before she went on. "She has only lived here a couple of years. When she first came, she sat in the cafeteria with me a few times. It—it was when I was running around with that bunch, you know, and was all mixed up. She got to know some of them, too. The trouble is nobody cared enough about her to steer her into a different group. I mean, you all worked on me. If she'd had a friend like you, she might be different today. I want to be that kind of friend to her now. I thought maybe the two of us could be friendly to her even if she never acts friendly."

Peggy knew Alice was waiting for her reply, but she couldn't squeeze an answer past the lump in her throat. First Bob, then Bill, and now Alice had looked beyond the green and purple eye shadow and recognized a cry for help. And all she had done was criticize.

"Do you think we could?" Alice asked again, her voice anxious.

Peggy cleared her throat enough to answer, "I'm with you on it. We've always said that miracles do happen."

# 5

**P**eggy had learned not to admit that she liked the excitement of getting back to school after summer vacation. This senior year, especially, should be fun. It would be a snap, with only four subjects instead of the five she'd carried the other three years, and one a reading course.

"Imagine getting credit toward graduation for taking something you're crazy about doing anyway," she exclaimed to Ellen.

But Ellen by the end of the first week was already moaning about the work that had piled up for her. "I always thought your senior year would be the easiest, but not with my schedule."

"It always seems hard at first until you get back in the groove of studying," Peggy reminded her, not really understanding how anyone could get so uptight over school. It was funny that her two best friends both panicked so easily over studies. For Alice, a C was an unexpected delight, and for Ellen it was a normal grade.

"Are you going out for any clubs this year?" Ellen's question jogged Peggy out of her thoughts.

"Oh, just the usual. Same as last year—French club, teacher's association. I'm on the paper again. I'd love to try out for the drill team, but I know I'd never make it."

"I guess I'll have to join something this year." Ellen's voice was so gloomy that Peggy couldn't help laughing at her.

"Don't do it if it's such a chore. Nobody's making you. You know you always say you hate to join something just to join."

"Yeah, but when my mother found out this summer that I haven't belonged to anything in all three years, she really tore the place apart. She asked if I wanted my bare name to stand out in the yearbook all by itself—Ellen Todd—with nothing to soften it, not even a middle name? Although I don't know how a middle name would help. She couldn't understand why I wasn't at least a member of the rec club, since I like sports so much. I told her I would be if they ever did anything worthwhile."

"Have you ever been to a meeting?"

"Once. The faculty advisor and the girls sat around and discussed the fine points of how to serve the birdie in starting a game of badminton. Why didn't they go out and sock it around awhile? That's the best way to learn. What a waste of time!"

Peggy laughed as usual at Ellen's pretense of being such a lone wolf. Yet it wasn't pretense, because that's the way she was. She didn't seem to need people or mind standing on the fringe of a group. Belonging just to belong wasn't important to her. *Life would be easier if I could be like that*, Peggy thought wistfully. A person wouldn't get so torn up inside if she didn't care so much.

She smiled back at Ellen then. "So anyway, you're joining this year just for the way it will look in the yearbook," she teased.

"Just for the way my *mother* wants it to look," Ellen retorted. "I couldn't care less. The trick is to find out how seldom you can attend meetings and still be considered a member."

"You don't do that with church meetings," Peggy said. "Seems to me you're there whenever something is going on."

"That's different. Church is one of the most important parts of my life." And Peggy knew that, for

Ellen, that was practically a maudlin statement.

As the weeks slowly accumulated and the hot September days drifted into an unusually warm October, Peggy was glad her school schedule was easy. Life was so busy she would have been swamped if she had had to spend a lot of time studying. She was sorry now that she had agreed to be on call whenever the store needed extra help, because she found herself working more often than she wanted to.

At least the work was interesting, since she never knew from one time to the next what she would be doing. Sometimes she checked stock in the basement, counting boxes of this and that, and sometimes she filled the shelves with needed items, neither of them very imaginative jobs. It was more fun to capture the slow-moving turtles and wiggly goldfish and put them into small containers for wide-eyed children, or help choose candles and napkins and prizes for birthday parties. She didn't even mind being on the cash register so much anymore. But she did hate working at the lunch counter.

At first, she just helped clean up the dishes and get the steam table in shape for the next day's business. It wasn't glamorous work, but there was something satisfying about seeing the shining chrome and sparkling glasses when she finished cleaning.

But she did hate it when she had to fill in for someone and wait on customers and take orders. She never could think of a snappy answer to the wisecracks that came her way.

"You're too serious," one of the regular girls said one day. "Yak with those guys a little. They usually leave a bigger tip if you give them a smart answer back."

"I didn't know anyone tipped at a lunch counter." She couldn't hide her surprise. "None of the kids do that I know."

"Oh, the high school kids!" the girl retorted in amused disgust. "Not them, no. Most of them squeeze out fifty or sixty cents for a soft drink and then sit there waiting for change. I'm talking about the older guys who come in for pie and coffee or a sandwich. If you're friendly, they'll usually throw down something. Every dime helps."

Peggy worked the lunch counter regularly after school started, and the others left the high school crowd to her as often as they could. Since the store was close to school, it got the crowd first for cold drinks before the kids moved on to the fast-food places.

The manager had asked Peggy to work every afternoon and Friday evening the second week of October. Peggy had hesitated, thinking of the party they had planned at church for Friday. Then she had agreed, remembering that she might need this job during vacations. Her college fund was still pretty skimpy.

On Tuesday she saw Phyllis, with Roy and Mike trailing, come in and grab the end seats at the counter, which partially hid them from the store manager's view. Peggy had heard him give them a curt order more than once not to take up room too long for just a soft drink.

Peggy went over with her order book, though she knew she could remember what they wanted without having to write it down. While she listened, two other guys from school sat down next to Roy and added their cokes to the order she wrote down.

She reached for glasses and filled them generously with ice, trying not to listen to the thought whispering a reminder that she owed Phyllis an invitation. She tried to shut it out, but couldn't. The combined unspoken rebuke in Bob and Bill's voices and her agreement with Alice echoed in her ears. She took their order to them, collected their money,

41

and returned with change. Then she began to wipe the already clean counter, uncomfortably aware of the intent look of Phyllis's gray eyes.

She hated to ask her in front of Roy and Mike and hoped the other two guys would leave first. But when she glanced along the counter and saw other customers waiting, she knew she couldn't wait. She said, in what she hoped was a casual, offhand tone, "By the way, we've got another party coming up Friday at church. How about coming?"

"Not another one of those!" Peggy didn't know whether it was Roy or Mike who gave the jeering answer. She ignored him and went on looking at Phyllis, sure that she was the one who made the decisions. If she wanted to do something, the guys probably tagged along without too many objections.

"You'll like it," she urged, hoping her voice carried more confidence than she really felt. She hoped, too, that the smile she had pasted on her lips looked more friendly than she felt.

"We won't like it unless it's got more going for it than that other thing we got hooked into," the same guy said.

Peggy didn't answer, still waiting for Phyllis to decide. She knew the other two guys sitting at the counter were watching and listening, but she didn't dare look at them. She knew if she did, and saw them laughing, she would run. Ordinarily she would have retreated by now, but this time she was determined to carry it through. They had already laughed at her, wich was all they could do. And anyway, their opinion wasn't so great. This was an angle she hadn't thought of before, and it gave her extra courage.

"Think you can make it?" she asked again. "It starts at seven thirty."

"Will Bill be there?" Phyllis's bold eyes stared at her, and Peggy stared right back.

"He and Candy are planning the games."

"Games!" mocked one of the boys—Roy, Peggy thought. "You want us to help pin the tail on the donkey and drop the hankerchief?"

"Why don't you come and find out?" Peggy snapped back at him. "Don't knock something until you've tried it." She looked at him defiantly and then back at Phyllis. "It's Friday at seven thirty at the church. The big white one on the corner of Elm and Second."

She turned and walked away and began polishing the glasses so furiously that one of the girls suggested she'd better quit while there was something left. She felt silly when she realized that her hands were shaking. *What would I have done if I'd been standing in front of lions in a Roman arena like Christians way back when did?* she wondered. Still, even this was a victory for her, and she hoped she would remember it the next time she was tempted to chicken out.

But Thursday she knew she had muffed another chance. Mr. Doty had given an impromptu assignment at the beginning of the hour to write three hundred words on "My Philosophy of Life" and gave them the hour to do it. Peggy wrote furiously, trying to satisfy Mr. Doty's philosophical and intellectual standards. When she finished and read it over quickly, she knew almost anyone could have signed his name to the paper. Nothing in it was hers alone.

"If I'd only had sense enough to write what I really believe," she mourned to Ellen and Alice as they stood in line in the cafeteria. "Instead I beat around the bush and ended up with a lot of fancy words that don't say anything."

"Yes, but it's awfully hard to write on a subject like that," Alice sympathized.

"The subject isn't so bad," Ellen said. "But three hundred words! How could you stretch it out so long?"

43

"Well, Mr. Doty wants you to go into an explanation of how you feel destiny is working out the events of your life in accordance with the meshing of forces and stuff like that."

"Why?" Ellen asked. "Why can't you just say that you believe God made the world for a purpose and that you think He has a plan for your life? Doesn't Mr. Parker say things like that? Of course, you'd have to pad it a lot because that wouldn't take any three hundred words."

"But you can't be that direct, not in a paper," Peggy objected. "You have to be more subtle, not so blunt."

"Why?" Ellen asked again.

"Because—" Peggy stopped and looked at Ellen's genuinely puzzled face "—to get a better grade, I guess," she finished weakly.

"You mean, he grades you by what he believes? That isn't fair!"

"I don't know that he does. But I guess I thought he might. Well, it's too late now to change this paper. Somebody says he does this twice a year, so next time I'll write what I really believe." She stopped to grin at Ellen. "Even if it isn't three hundred words."

She looked to see what was offered for lunch. "Ugh! Tomato soup! How can anyone stand that stuff?"

The girl in line ahead of her hesitated, her hand hovering over a bowl of soup. Then she reached for the last plate of fruit salad.

"Why didn't I keep still?" she muttered to Ellen. "The salad was what I wanted. Guess I'll have to take a bowl of chili."

When they came to class on Friday, Mr. Doty looked at them over his glasses and spent fifteen minutes on a stern lecture about the general fuzziness in the thinking of the modern generation.

Then he said, "I'm going to pass out these themes, and I want each of you to take one, making sure you don't have your own. First read it through to yourself. Then call on the person who wrote it to explain in one sentence what he thinks he said in his paper."

Like everyone else, Peggy was more interested in trying to see who had her paper than in reading the one she had received, but she didn't recognize her writing on any of the papers near her. Mr. Doty gave five minutes for silent reading and then started at the front of the room. Peggy sighed with relief every time someone else's name was called, and kept an apprehensive eye on the clock. The hour had never seemed so long before. Finally she concentrated on the paper before her. After reading it through twice, she realized that she had no idea what the person was trying to say. She knew from the name that it was a girl like Alice who really struggled for grades. But even so, Mr. Doty *was* right when he got mad at fuzzy thinking.

*Maybe if I weren't so hungry, this would make more sense,* she thought. *This hour before lunch is always so long. I could even eat tomato soup today.*

The thought was only half-formed when yesterday's incident came back. Because *she* had had an opinion about tomato soup, and had expressed it, she had changed someone else's mind. Peggy felt as though a window had opened suddenly, letting in dazzling light. Why couldn't she be just as positive about something as important as her faith?

And then a Bible verse came out of nowhere with sudden impact. She had read it one day a long time ago when she was just leafing through the Bible, looking at words. Because she loved words and the pictures they made in her mind, she had read this verse, Jeremiah 15:16, over and over. "Your words were found, and I ate them, and Your word was to

45

me the joy and rejoicing of my heart." If that really was what God's Word was to her, why should she be ashamed to say so?

Then she heard her name called by someone sitting two seats ahead of her. As he looked around, she thought he was one of the two guys sitting near Phyllis in the store Tuesday. He was a reminder that she had had the courage to speak to Phyllis, and it hadn't been so hard. She could do it again now.

So with clammy hands and a slight quaver in her voice, she said, "My philosophy of life is based on Jesus Christ, who is my Savior from sin and who gives me peace in this life and eternal security for the future."

She realized as she heard the words herself that they were almost a direct quote from something Mr. Parker had said in church recently. But they did express her own feelings, too.

The words seemed to hang in the room, she thought, until Mr. Doty looked at the one who had her paper. "Is that what she has written there?"

He looked down at the paper for a moment and then shook his head. "This has got a lot of big, fancy words, but it sure doesn't say that."

Mr. Doty nodded. "All of your papers prove a point I want to get across to you and hope you will remember. Be direct when you write. I'm not interested this much—" and the loud snap of his fingers rang in the room "—in whether you hold the same opinions I do. But you had an hour to chew the end of your pen and think about what to say. And what was the result? You all came up with pretentious, vague words, showing that most of you don't know what—if anything—you believe. You used twenty or thirty words just to get to three hundred, when one or two would have been sufficient."

He launched into a lecture on writing. Peggy, half-listening to his familiar theme, told herself sternly to remember this lesson. After all, it didn't bother her to say she hated tomato soup and loved pizza and apricots. Why couldn't she just as freely say she hated sin and loved God?

# 6

Peggy raced to her locker after the last class and twirled the combination lock expertly, then opened the door cautiously. She turned as she heard Alice laughing behind her. "If you could see the way you look when you do that!"

"Listen! I've been cracked on the head so many times by the junk that comes pelting down from that top shelf that I never yank the door open unless I'm hidden behind it."

"Haven't you seen how I've reformed this year? Haven't you noticed how neat the locker looks?"

"I'm not admitting anything until the end of the year," Peggy retorted. "I've shared a locker with you too long to expect miracles."

"Then why, when they announced that seniors could have separate lockers, did you choose to stay with me?"

Peggy grinned back. "You know how hard it is to break a bad habit."

Alice reached for the books she needed. "Are you working this afternoon?"

"Uh-huh. That's why I'm rushing now. And tonight, too, so I'll be late for the party."

"You want someone to come pick you up?"

"No. My dad said he'd get me right at nine and run me over. I'm just going to wear this outfit, even though it's kind of dressy for the party. Thanks anyway." Peggy stacked the books she needed on

48

top of her notebook and flipped a sweater over her arm. "I've got to run, or I'll be late."

"Look, let me take your books home for you so you won't have to lug them along to the store and then have to remember them after work."

"I don't want to bother you. You've got a stack of your own. Or is Dan walking with you?"

Peggy caught the flicker of hesitation before Alice said, "He'll be along in a minute. We can detour by your house and drop them off."

"OK, if you're sure it's no trouble. Thanks a lot." She raced down the stairs, thinking that at least all her rushing kept her from getting fat.

She made it to the store with a couple of minutes to spare and was glad to be put on taking inventory of the Christmas stock. It was a simple matter to total the number of boxes of dolls, puzzles, and games and imagine the delighted faces of little kids when they opened these boxes. She didn't mind being isolated and surrounded by stacks of boxes, because it left her time to daydream. Then, at five-fifteen, the assistant manager told her to take a supper break and get ready to work one of the cash registers for the business that usually poured in on Friday evenings.

She still feel a little nervous at the responsibility, even though one of the girls said the machine did most of the thinking. "Of course," she added with an expressive shrug of her shoulders, "if there's a mistake, the machine doesn't get the blame. We do."

The rush had just begun when a man came with a load of stuff and dumped it on her counter. Peggy rang up the prices of the paint brushes, rolls of tape, flashlight batteries, small boxes of nails of various sizes, and four long curtain rods. She put everything into one big sack and handed him the odd-shaped parcel, smiling up at him. Then a puzzled line etched her forehead as she looked at his familiar face, wondering if she should know him from church. Aware of her intent look, he fumbled his wallet back into his pocket, grabbed the package, and left quickly.

His embarrassed expression brought the immediate recollection of where she had seen him. She turned, wanting to call after him, "It *was* a five-dollar bill that woman gave me," but she didn't. She was sure he had known it at the time.

The rush of customers kept her so busy that it was closing time before she realized it. As she took her money box to the office, she suddenly realized that she was bushed, there was a party going on at church, and that she didn't care.

*When Dad comes for me, I think I'll just go straight home,* she decided, and went to the women's restroom to comb her hair. She surveyed herself in the mirror with frowning distaste, seeing the smudges of tiredness under her eyes and the droop of her shoulders. She knew she and Ellen and some of the other usually dateless girls would end up sticking together all evening anyway, and that wasn't an exciting thought, much as she liked Ellen. It would be better to go straight home, since she had missed most of the party anyway.

She stepped out of the store into a drizzling rain and looked for her father from the shelter of the doorway. A car honked at the curb down the street and she heard Ellen call, "Hey, Peggy!"

Holding her purse over her head to protect her hair, she dashed for the car and slid in through the open door. "What are you doing here?" Then, as Ellen backed out of the parking place without answering, she said, "Wait! My dad's coming for me."

"No, he's not. I called him and said I'd get you."

"You shouldn't have bothered," Peggy protested. "You didn't have to leave the party just for me."

"I haven't been there yet. We had unexpected company for dinner. They were people we used to know way back when. Their daughter was supposedly my best friend when I was about two, so I had to stay. They only left about ten minutes ago, and I called your house to see when you would be through working. If you hadn't been going late, I wouldn't have come at all."

"And here I was all set to go home with my dad and get to bed early. I'm beat, and the idea of a party leaves me cold."

Ellen slowed in front of the church parking lot. "Well, we don't have to go—"

Peggy gave a tired gesture. "As long as we're here, let's see what's happening. We can leave early if you want to."

"Let's hope it's worth the effort," Ellen answered. She looked around the parking lot in surprise. "There are a lot of cars, so there must be a lot of people."

They could tell the party was still in full swing as soon as they walked into the room. Peggy was immediately grabbed for a trivia game, both sides wanting her. "We're on the literature category, and everybody's stuck. Come on, you'll know all the quotes, and authors, and titles, and everything."

When the game was over, Peggy finally had a chance to look around to see who was there. She saw six or eight of the new kids who had been at the earlier party, but not Phyllis or her two shadows. Peggy was disappointed. Her invitation hadn't counted for anything after all.

Then from behind her, someone said, "Hi. I thought at first I'd come to the wrong church when I didn't see you here. But you did say the corner of Elm and Second."

She turned and saw the fellow from lit class who had had her theme that morning. "I did?" she repeated blankly.

51

"Don't you remember?" His grin was friendly and was reflected in the deep blue of his eyes as he looked down at her intently.

"Who invited you? I mean—how did you know about the party? I mean, are you sure it was me— I?" She smiled back at him, but inside she was furious at herself for sounding so dumb.

"Don't you remember? I sat in on your invitation to what's-her-name, the one who looks like an ad for a paint company. I could tell she probably wasn't going to take you up on it, and I thought someone should since you were so persistent."

Again his grin was slow and friendly, and this time admiring, as he added, "Besides, I liked your answer in class this morning."

"Why?" she asked, hearing the unaccustomed pertness in her voice. "Because it got Mr. Doty started on one of his pet lectures, and he didn't get around to your paper?"

He nodded back. "Partly that. But I was thinking I'd have to give that kind of an answer, because I thought someone should. I just transferred in this fall and don't know many people in school yet. I didn't know anyone else in the class was a Christian, and nothing in your paper let me know you were." His easy smile that crinkled laugh lines around his eyes took the sting out of his words.

It made her say frankly, but with an embarrassed flush, "I find it awfully hard to talk about my faith to people who don't think the same way I do. Especially teachers. So it really meant a lot to me to get up enough courage to say what I did."

"I know what you mean," he agreed. "It's kind of hard to stick out like a sore thumb. But if we really believe something, we shouldn't be afraid to admit it."

Peggy was aware then that Ellen had come over and was nudging her surreptitiously. "Do you know

Ellen Todd? This is—" She stopped, trying to dredge up his name. Mr. Doty *must* have called on him in class sometime during the last month, but she had no idea what his name was.

"That's OK." He smiled at her confusion. "I didn't know yours until I saw it on your theme this morning. I'm John Stewart."

"You've probably met a lot of others by now," Peggy said as she gestured around the room.

He nodded. "At least I've heard a bunch of names. Some of them I knew, like Dan Schwartz. We're generally somewhere together alphabetically. But I didn't know he went to church anywhere."

There was an odd note of something in his voice, and Peggy looked at him, puzzled by it. But he was going on, "And that's—what's her name? The girl with him. Alice something."

"Alice Matthews," Peggy answered and couldn't keep down the familiar stab of envy as she looked across the room at Alice. With her around, what chance did any other girl have to get a guy's interest? She gave John a sidelong glance and saw him still looking in Alice's direction. With a trace of bitterness she thought that as usual, and without even trying, Alice had caught his attention.

Then she was startled to hear him say, "I've seen her around and thought she must be a Christian." In answer to her look of surprise, he asked, "You don't think so?"

"Oh, she is!"

"No, I mean, don't you think she looks like one?"

"How can you tell?" Ellen asked, her voice curious.

"Well—" He stopped, obviously hunting for words, and frowned across the room to where Alice stood talking to Dan. Peggy wished she could change the subject, because it suddenly hit her that he had just indirectly admitted that he hadn't known she was a Christian.

"How come you know about Alice?" Ellen persisted in her usual direct way when she wanted to know something.

John turned to answer her question. "She looks like the kind you'd vote in as homecoming queen, doesn't she? You know, you can just see her with a crown and a robe and carrying an armful of roses like Miss America. Sometimes girls like that who get a lot of attention for the way they look don't care about other people. They want everyone to be interested in them."

He looked across at Alice again. "But I've seen her around the halls at school. You can tell she's interested in people just for themselves—like those three kids you talked to," he said, looking down at Peggy. "I'm not saying that only Christians are interested in other people, but we *should* be. And she is."

"Yeah," Ellen agreed slowly, and then more enthusiastically, "that's Alice exactly! You're pretty sharp for being the new guy on the block."

Peggy noticed how one of his eyebrows quirked in a funny way as he grinned back at Ellen's snappy answer. "It was the tea leaves that did it. I always read personalities that way."

"You'll have to settle for cold drinks or cocoa tonight," Peggy said. "Looks like the food is ready."

She had a sharp feeling of disappointment when John strolled over and joined a bunch of boys instead of following her and Ellen in the line. Then she scolded herself for trying to make a big deal out of a casual conversation.

Thinking back on the party the next day, she found herself alternating between hope and anxiety. Now, in the cold light of the usual Saturday morning's scrubbing and vacuuming, the thought that John had seemed interested in her was utterly ridiculous. She had felt so grubby after the evening's work and had looked so horrible with her stringy hair and tired face. If she had only gone home first and put on some makeup and a sharper outfit. And then she had sounded so dumb when they talked.

Yet, she remembered, he had sort of hung around her—and Ellen, since they were together. He got a plate of food and a can of pop and then joined the group she was eating with. She had been able to find out scraps of information about him without having to ask directly herself.

Answering one of Bill's questions, he said, "You won't believe this, but I'm practically from a one-room schoolhouse. Our town is so small that there were only fifteen in last year's senior class. My dad decided we needed more competition, so we moved here about a month ago."

"Who's 'we'?" someone asked.

"My little sister and I. She's eight."

Peggy thought there was an unusually protective note in his voice when he talked about his sister, and wondered why, and hoped she would get to know him better. But when she looked around the group at the large ratio of girls to boys, she sighed. There was too much competition here. Especially Alice.

Then they found during the brief devotional time after they ate that he was a match for Ann at the piano. Lois didn't know the song the quartet wanted to play, and John said, "Hey, I think I know that one."

When they finished the number, Bill said, "How about playing with us regularly?"

John shook his head. "I can't do what Lois can," and smiled across at her. Watching, Peggy wondered how he could have known that Lois needed him to say that.

Bill said, "We've tried to get her to accompany us, but haven't persuaded her yet. Why don't you come in with us temporarily, anyhow. We need someone to cover our mistakes."

"You guys don't need anyone to cover you. You're good!" he exclaimed.

*He certainly is a lot like Bill,* Peggy thought now as she remembered snatches of things she had overheard him say as he talked with some of the other kids. It sounded as though he thought everything for a Christian was either yes or no, black or white, with no gray shades in between.

"When a person becomes a Christian, he should automatically live the way God wants him to. He tells us there are things we should do and things we shouldn't do."

In the quick heated discussion that followed, Peggy saw Dan's face as he sat on the edge of the group. The scorn in his eyes as he looked at John was so clear that it was almost as though he had shouted a sneering challenge. She had looked back at John uncertainly. Would he be as confident of his answers if Dan did argue with him?

She sat back on her heels to survey the freshly waxed kitchen floor, glad that Dan had shrugged himself into his jacket and taken Alice home without saying anything to John. She tried to remember what John looked like and smiled as the usual description of tall, dark, and handsome came to mind.

Then she slumped onto the floor, feeling defeated. What reason did she have to think anything at all would come of this? Just because a guy, new to the group, had talked to her because she was the only girl there that he knew even slightly, didn't mean that any kind of relationship would develop.

But the answer came back in the reminder that she had surrendered to God this longing to be liked in a special way by someone, and she was waiting for His answer.

# 7

She was so lost in her thoughts that she was startled when her mother from behind her said, "Mail for you. It came early today."

Peggy took the letter and glanced at the return address. "A great lot of mail this is. Just information from some college I never heard of. I wonder how I got on their mailing list."

"Perhaps they send literature to all high school seniors."

Peggy nodded as she skimmed the typewritten sheet and glanced over the enclosed forms. "Yes, that's all it is. Well, this is easy to get rid of," she said, tossing it into the wastebasket.

"Maybe you'd better keep it for a while," her mother suggested. "You might decide to go there."

"Not to that one! It's a private girls' school. I can't imagine why they would even need to send out a letter. Anyway, it probably costs a small fortune to go there."

"Have you thought definitely of where you do want to go?" The words were casual enough, but the note of anxiety in her mother's voice puzzled Peggy.

She decided to ignore it as she answered, "No—I have thought about the college where Ann is. I know I've got to make up my mind soon. It seems so far in the future, but it isn't really. The touble is, it's going to cost so much," she finished gloomily.

"We'll manage that somehow," her mother answered.

Peggy looked at her, sure that something serious was bothering her mother. There had to be some reason she was sitting around on a Saturday morning, doing nothing. She wondered how she could find out what it was without coming right out and asking.

Then her mother said, "At least you and Bill won't be starting the same year. That will help some."

And suddenly Peggy was sure her mother wasn't concerned about her choice of college but about where Bill would go. She wanted to answer her mother's unspoken question by saying, "Bill really wants to go to a college where he'll get a lot of Bible teaching." But she decided to sidestep the issue and not say anything. Bill could fight his own battles on that subject better than she could.

Then, prompted by an inner compulsion, she made her voice sound warm and gentle as she said, "It's really something, isn't it, the way he is so sure of the future. I mean, lots of boys his age are still kids, just goofing off without any purpose in life. But Bill—well, he knows exactly what he wants to be, and he's got it all mapped out how to get there."

"I hope he has given up this ridiculous idea of being a missionary." Mrs. Andrews's voice was low and even, but Peggy could feel the tension behind the words. She wanted desperately to give an answer that would help her mother understand Bill's plans.

But there seemed nothing else to do but meet her mother's words head on, so she said just as quietly and evenly, "No, Mother, he hasn't. He is sure that's what God wants him to do."

"I'm tired of hearing that kind of talk!" Mrs. Andrews lashed out in bitter anger. "It's absolutely foolish for him to hold onto a silly childish notion like that now that he's old enough to know better."

"It isn't just a silly notion," Peggy began.

But her mother went on without giving any sign that she had heard the interruption. "I certainly blame the church and Mr. Parker for encouraging him in this idea of throwing his life away. And your father and you as well. Probably Ed encouraged him while he lived there. He listens to everyone but me on this matter. I'm surprised you aren't planning the same foolishness!" She threw the words out scornfully in a blaze of anger.

Peggy chose her words carefully as she answered, "No, I think I really want to be a teacher. But I think God can use Christian teachers—"

"Why can't Bill see that?" her mother interrupted fiercely. "Can't God—if you want to put it that way—use him as a lawyer, or in business, or in some other respectable profession?"

"Mother! It's respectable to be a missionary!"

"Not for *my* son," Mrs. Andrews answered coldly. "And I certainly cannot understand how you and your father can encourage him."

Peggy looked at her mother, feeling helpless, not wanting to argue and make the situation worse. Yet she didn't want to leave anything unsaid that might help her mother understand. Two years ago, even a year ago, she knew she would have flared in anger at her mother's attitude and would have sat in tight-lipped silence. But now she felt compassion for her mother as she tried to look at this from her viewpoint. Her mother had had to give up Jane when she was still a baby. Naturally she would think that still another of her children was being taken from her. And by a God whom she refused to acknowledge.

So, from where she still sat in the kitchen doorway, her back braced against the door frame and

59

her hands tightly clasped around her knees, she tried to speak slowly and carefully.

"I don't think either Bill or I have been very good at living what we believe, or you would understand how he feels about this. The most important thing anyone can do in this life is to accept Christ as his Savior. But then you have to live for Him, too, and tell others about Him. Bill wouldn't be happy doing anything else, Mother. Don't try to stop him or make him feel bad about his wanting to. Please?"

Her mother's always erect figure seemed to sag a little as she looked back at Peggy's pleading look. Then she straightened and said coldly, "You know very well that I will let him make his own choices even though I have no sympathy whatever with his ideas. I had hoped that my son would make a name for himself in this world. He has the ability to be a person of influence and importance. But I suppose if he is determined to throw his life away, there is nothing I can do about it. I can only hope that he will come to his senses before it is too late."

As Peggy started to protest, she went on more firmly. "No, Peggy, please don't press the point with me. I know perfectly well what you and your father and Bill believe. I have never tried to interfere in this madness that has affected the three of you, but I do not want it for myself."

She stopped and seemed lost in thought. Then in a tired and defeated voice, she finished, "I never thought the day would come when I would be glad that Emily and I were on the same side. But it has."

Peggy swallowed hard past the lump that filled her throat at both the anger and the sadness in her mother's voice. Finally she said softly, "I have to tell you that I've been praying for you and Aunt Emily for a long time."

Mrs. Andrews stood up abruptly and turned sharply away. "Don't do it! I don't want you to!"

Peggy watched her mother's slender, unyielding figure as she walked upstairs to her room. She thought how many times through the years her mother had sought refuge in her bedroom, trying to escape the bitterness and frustration of her life. Once again she felt a closeness with her mother and shared her loneliness. But at the same time she ached for her mother to understand that God could be her refuge.

Thoughts about her mother filled her mind so completely that she didn't watch the time. She answered the phone when it rang and heard Alice ask, "Are you working at all today?"

"Thanks for calling! Yes! I'm supposed to be there at twelve, and I'm a mess."

"I'll meet you and catch the bus, too. Or are you driving?"

"No, it's too much trouble to park. I'll meet you at quarter to—no, make it eleven-thirty." Peggy corrected herself to make allowance for Alice's usual lateness. But by the time she had dashed around, eating a sandwich while she dressed, it was almost a quarter to twelve when she reached the corner.

"We just missed a bus, so we'd better walk. You've got time, haven't you, if we walk fast?" Alice started off and added, "I really didn't expect to find you home when I called. I thought you worked mornings too."

"I go late on days after I work the evening shift," Peggy explained. "Believe me, I can use that extra sleep on Saturday."

"Especially when you go to a party after work and the best looking guy there follows you around all evening."

Alice's voice was perfectly serious, but Peggy looked at her quickly to see if she was joking. "Did—did you think so, too?" she asked, her voice rising

61

in a squeak of disbelieving excitement. "I mean, it wasn't just my imagination?"

"Of course it wasn't," Alice assured her, and Peggy sighed with relief.

"I'd just about convinced myself that I was building something out of nothing when I thought about it this morning. I didn't want to say anything to Ellen on the way home last night because it sounded conceited. And anyway, he talked to Ellen as much as he did to me. And when Bill didn't make any typical brotherly comments at breakfast this morning, I was sure it was just wishful thinking."

She stopped, wondering if Alice could really understand why this was such a big thing with her. Alice's problem had always been having too many dates instead of none at all.

But Alice said, "You were the only one he paid any attention to at all, Peg. As soon as you came in, he made a beeline for you. And he's *so* good looking!"

"Did Dan say anything to you about him after the party?"

"No. Why?"

"He said he knew Dan, so I thought maybe Dan might have said something about him." She let the words drag off because she didn't want to bring up the disdain she had seen on Dan's face when he listened to John.

But now she did notice the slight hesitation before Alice lifted her shoulders in a slight shrug and said, "No, he didn't. You know how Dan is."

Peggy wanted to say, "No, I don't. And I wonder if *anyone* really knows what he is thinking." But she didn't ask any questions. Alice was so loyal to her friends that no one could pry anything out of her that she didn't think she should tell. Peggy couldn't help wondering what was wrong with Dan lately. It must be something more than his usual conceit, because Alice certainly must be used to that by now. Whatever was wrong with him was bothering her.

But right now, with her heart singing, she couldn't think about anything sad. With Alice's reassurances ringing in her ears, everything was wonderful. She could even look forward to working all afternoon and coping with the Saturday rush.

Alice had bolstered her hopes so much that she couldn't keep down an absurd ache of disappointment when John didn't phone that evening. She had to remind herself sternly that she was making something big out of a few friendly words. *Don't scare him off by overreacting,* she told herself sternly.

Since John had said his family was still visiting different churches in town, trying to decide which one to settle in, she didn't expect to see him on Sunday. But when she got out of the car with Ellen in the evening, she felt her heart pound at the sight of his tall figure in the group of boys that was standing on the front steps. It took superhuman effort to be casual in her attitude and offhand in her responses to him then and after the service.

John stopped beside her as everyone stood talking in the crisp air. "I'm going to try to convince my parents that this is the church we should come to. Fortunately they won't need much convincing."

"How do they know about it? Isn't this the first time you've been here? To a service I mean," she added with a smile.

"Second. We were here once last month but only in the morning." Peggy was so busy wondering why she hadn't seen him that she lost what he was saying and only picked up the end of his sentence, "—they like Mr. Parker's friendliness."

"Are they here tonight?" she asked, trying to find people who might look like him.

"I came by myself. I thought I owed it to everyone since I crashed the party the other night."

"Oh, crashed!" she protested. "And anyway, you claim to have been invited."

"I was, indirectly." He smiled down at her. As he did, she couldn't help the thought that flashed into her mind. What if she hadn't made herself give that invitation to Phyllis? Would she have met him some other way? Was this God's way of rewarding her? She shook off the confusing thoughts and decided just to be glad for what was happening.

She caught sight of her father coming down the steps. In answer to the questioning lift of his eyebrows, she shook her head. "I'll come home with Ellen," she called. "My dad," she said in explanation to John and saw him nod.

"I saw you sitting with him the other time I was here. Is Bill the only other one in your family?"

She nodded and then said quickly, "Except my mother, of course."

"He can really make that trumpet talk."

"He is good," she admitted. "But it took effort to get that way, not only on his part but from the rest of us. *We* had to listen. Believe me, he didn't always sound the way he does now."

Ellen came along then with a shivering, "Brr, it's getting colder. Ready, Peg?"

She nodded and turned reluctantly. She was still afraid this was all a dream, and that she would wake up and find she was still outside the magic circle, a solitary figure on the edge of an enchanted world.

But as the days slipped by, she found it wasn't a dream. John began to walk with her to her locker after lit class. Then the pattern took shape, and he walked her home or to the store the days she worked, and took her to the games. Now when the phone rang in the evening she sprang to answer, sure that at least one call would be from him. And she was never disappointed.

Bill and the others in the quartet had persuaded him to accompany them whenever they played in public. This meant that he also rehearsed with them.

"Why don't you guys ever practice here?" Peggy asked one evening when Bill came home from Jim's house.

"What's with all the sisterly interest?" he asked in mock surprise. "After all the complaints we've heard about the racket we make, I should think you'd be glad we practice someplace else. There must be an added attraction all of a sudden." He grinned at her.

Peggy pretended indifference. "OK, so bother the Parkers. I just thought it wasn't fair to inflict the noise on them all the time." But as her eyes met Bill's she couldn't help laughing.

"I don't suppose you'd be interested in knowing what he said about you?" Bill asked casually.

Not even bothering to pretend that she didn't know whom he meant, she asked eagerly, "What?"

"Um—no, I'd better not tell you. It might blow you up too much."

"Bill! Tell me."

"Now wait a minute! How can you be so sure it's something you want to hear?"

"Because John doesn't go around saying things about people unless it's something complimentary."

"John? Is that who we're talking about?" Then he grinned. "OK. It didn't really amount to so much. He just said that if he believed in going steady, he'd like to go steady with you. Naturally I told him you wouldn't consider it—"

He broke off at Peggy's indignant and alarmed, "Bill! You didn't! You wouldn't do that to me!"

"He wouldn't have believed me anyway," Bill went on calmly. "With you falling over yourself and hanging on every word he says to show him you like him, he'd have to be blind—"

"I don't either. I don't do that, do I?"

He relented then with a grin. "I'm kidding. But not about what he said," he added quickly. "He did say he liked you."

"Really? You're serious now?"

He nodded. "And he's really a neat guy, Peg. One of the best around now that Larry and Bob are gone."

# 8

**P**eggy could measure the depth of satisfaction she found in dating John by the bubbling happiness that woke her every morning and sent her drifting off to sleep at night. And along with the happiness she had a quiet feeling of contentment. She had always before been frozen in tongue-tied confusion when she had to attempt a conversation with a boy. Now she found John to be the easiest person possible to talk to. She didn't have a feverish feeling of having to chatter on continually in order to hold his interest. And she found she didn't have to pretend to like something or not like something. She could just be herself.

She discovered this in a roundabout way soon after they started dating. At first, in her fear that she couldn't keep him interested in her, she tried so hard to be vivacious and entertaining every time they were together, that she felt worn out with the effort.

Then one Sunday evening, they all sat listening to the social committee debate what kind of party to plan. "Instead of planning something for *us*, how about doing something different? Why not put on a party for someone else?"

Everyone turned to look at John. "Who?"

"Isn't there a children's home someplace around that would let us come in and have a party for the kids? It's almost the end of October. Halloween is a natural time for a party for kids."

"Great idea!" Bill agreed. "Let's get committees going right away."

Since this was the first time they had planned something like this, the committees were a little slow getting started. John was chosen general chairman since the idea was his, and Peggy, Jim, and Ellen were picked to work with him.

Ellen phoned one day, her voice abrupt. "I've got a problem. Do you know Shirley, one of the new kids who's been coming all the time? Well, she wants to tell fortunes. Do you think she should? She said she did it at parties at another church she went to. I didn't know what to tell her."

"Let's ask Mrs. Springer," Peggy answered. "I'd be kind of leery of it myself. The grade school I went to had a carnival every October around Halloween and had a fortune-teller's booth. But—well, let's ask Mrs. Springer's advice."

When Ellen called back, she said, "Mrs. Springer asked if we could all come there. She's making the boys' costumes for a party at school, and she said she'd work while we talked. And she suggested maybe all the committee members should come so everyone could put in his two cents on this. OK? I'll pick you up at seven." Before Peggy could say anything, Ellen laughed. "I'm so used to saying that, I forgot you've got transportation. How about you and John picking me up?"

Peggy put down the phone and stood for a moment, tapping her fingers and frowning. Ellen's voice had been as breezy as usual, but was she really as unconcerned about dating as she seemed to be? Her own experiences of being the third person were so fresh in her mind that it made her sensitive to others in that situation. Some of the guys in the group were certainly blind not to see Ellen.

Ellen was waiting when John pulled up in front, and she got in the car before he could go around to open the door for her. She was obviously troubled by Shirley's offer and poured the whole story out to John. "And a couple of other girls want to dress like witches and then read the kids' horoscopes. My mother used to read hers and mine every day, until she got saved. She quit when she read that was something a Christian should never do, because only God knows the future."

"I think probably Mrs. Springer can help straighten it out. She's got some good ideas and usually doesn't mind giving them." John laughed. "She's already told me I need to learn what t-a-c-t spells."

As Peggy sat listening to the conversation in the big, colorful kitchen, she was impressed by the way Mrs. Springer was handling a touchy situation. Shirley and her friends were really uptight as they outlined their plans.

"I'm just going to tell the little girls that they'll be Miss America or something and tell the boys they'll be famous baseball or basketball players. What's wrong with that?"

"Will it be true?"

"Well—no—of course not—maybe they will—who knows—" She threw out her hands in frustration. "It's not really a lie. It's just in fun."

John had been leaning back in his chair listening and said slowly, "Kids sometimes don't know the difference."

Peggy looked at him, struck by an indefinable note in his voice, and she suddenly realized there was a lot she didn't know about him.

Mrs. Springer nodded, her face sober. "I know you planned this as a fun thing, Shirley. Perhaps I see it more seriously because I fear the unseen forces that are trying to capture my boys."

"What do you mean?" Ellen asked.

"Have you ever thought what Ephesians six is really saying?" She reached for her Bible on the ledge by the phone and handed it to John. "Read verses eleven and twelve."

"Put on the whole armor of God, that you may be able to stand against the wiles of the devil. For we do not wrestle against flesh and blood, but against principalities, against powers, against the rulers of the darkness of this age, against spiritual hosts of wickedness in the heavenly places."

When he finished reading, John said, "So it means we aren't fighting something we can see, some *thing*. It's not flesh and blood."

"Exactly. The devil is getting at Christians—did you realize that these verses are written to saved people?—in ways we don't suspect. One of the ways is by making us think horoscopes and fortune telling is just a lot of fun and that it's harmless. Anything that takes our minds away from the fact that only God can control the world is dangerous. Only He knows the end from the beginning."

Ellen said suddenly, "Is that why the boys don't have any E.T. or Superman, or Star Wars shirts or toys? I've wondered about that when I've sat with them."

Mrs. Springer nodded and gave a helpless shrug. "Many of my friends, even my church friends, think I'm terribly narrow. Oh, if someone comes to a birthday party and gives one of them a Star Wars toy or book, I don't snatch it away. We just don't buy them for the boys."

"I can understand the Star Wars thing with that 'May the force be with you' business," Shirley said. "That's something—I mean, only the Holy Spirit can be with us—isn't that right?"

Mrs. Springer smiled at her. "You are more perceptive than many of my adult friends."

"But, Superman! How come? He's always against evil. And in real life people—police—honest people fight against crime."

"Using supernatural means?"

"Well, no—"

"That's what I mean by the unseen forces trying to capture the minds of my children. You only have to read the reviews to see the many movies that are in the realm of the occult. All I ask is that you be discerning and on guard against anything, no matter how innocent it looks, that says in effect, 'God isn't so great. We can do anything that He can do.' "

Shirley gave a shaky laugh. "I guess I was planning to tell the girls they could be Miss America when maybe more of them want to be an astronaut—is that what women are called, too?—or President. Anyway, I won't do it. But then you've got to help with ideas you think are right for little kids."

"I'll suggest ideas and leave them for you to develop, but first help me clean out the extra food in the refrigerator."

The party the next week did click with the children, and they wore the costumes Mrs. Springer and the girls improvised for them, making each one of them a character from a children's book. The little boy who ended up as Piglet was everyone's favorite.

Peggy, susceptible as always to the sadness in a situation, had been quiet during the evening. She knew the children were taken care of physically and loved by the overworked staff. But the whole atmosphere depressed her. Maybe, she thought, it was only because she had worked all day and was tired. She didn't feel up to the effort of smiling just to smile and looking happy when she didn't feel happy.

She wondered if going with someone, as she was with John, always involved a certain amount of deceit. It *was* deceitful to pretend to be enthusiastic and vivacious when lots of times she would rather just be quiet and listen.

Her thoughts, a strange mixture of moodiness and contentment, kept her company all the way home, a background to the conversation swirling around her from those in the back seat. Finally, after taking three others home, John pulled into her driveway and came around to open the door for her. She looked up at him as she got out of the car. "Sorry I was such a dud tonight."

"Who wants someone bending his ear all the time?" John smiled back and then added, "Anyway, this is more your style, isn't it?"

She looked at him in surprise. "How did you know?"

"I didn't think you were the giddy, empty-headed type when I first saw you in lit class and when I heard you talking to Phyllis."

"You don't like the frivolous type?"

"Nope. Oh, sure, everybody wants to kid around and have a good time. I'm as ready for jokes and laughs as anyone. But there comes a time when you want to know where you stand with someone. And if that person thinks life is just one big party, well—" He shrugged. "You can't build much of a relationship that way."

Peggy felt a vast sense of relief wash over her. She sat down on the top step of the porch, with John leaning against the railing.

"One reason I couldn't say much tonight was seeing those kids. I felt so sorry for them. I know I would never make a good counselor, because I'd get so wrapped up in the people and their problems. I can't look at hurting people objectively."

"Those kids have got all they need. Don't you think so?" There was an oddly puzzling sound in the question, and Peggy looked up, trying to read his expression in the porch light.

"No! They don't have a home of their own with parents who love them."

72

"That's no guarantee that they'll be happy or even grow up to go the right way."

His tone was still searching, and Peggy wondered why. His parents were so united in everything. When she was at his house, she envied the way his mother showed her love for his dad so openly. The first time she had seen them hug each other, it had hit her that she had never seen her mother and father kiss each other.

She laced her fingers around her knees and stared out into the darkness. She had told John a little about their family problems and especially her concern about her mother's bitterness. He had listened sympathetically, but she wondered if he could really understand how the anxiety about her parents and the fear of their getting a divorce had colored her thinking. They no longer faced that problem, but the coolness, the distance between them, remained, and maybe always would. *At least until Mother becomes a Christian*, she thought now.

Then John's casual words shocked her, and she stared at him, not believing he had really said, "I was in a children's home until I was nine years old."

"You mean—the Stewarts aren't your real parents?"

He sat beside her on the step. "Yes, they are. But when I was two they separated and put—" he hesitated momentarily "—put me in a home. They didn't get a divorce, and they came sometimes to visit—me."

Again there was that slight hesitation before he went on, "I didn't think they would ever get back together again, and I thought I would have to live in the home forever. Or at least until I was sixteen, and then I'd have to make it on my own. I've had a feel for kids in a place like that ever since. That's why I wanted our group to do this party. If we wanted to, we could make a difference in those kids' lives, show them we care. It leaves a scar when you think you've been deserted."

"Well, you were!"

"Yeah, I suppose so. I thought so for a long time. Most of the kids were there because their parents were dead. But I always knew that—mine were living and just thought more about themselves than about—me. I was bitter for a long time."

"How did they get back together again?"

"My dad got saved and then my mother. Going back to live with them was rough at first. They had wiped out the mistakes of the past and thought we should, too. But it wasn't that easy. Then after I became a Christian, I finally could see it from their point of view and understand what had happened. They got married real young—had to, I guess."

He stopped to glance at her quickly and then away. "My dad was in college and had to drop out. He didn't have any training to get a decent job, so they didn't have any money. Neither of their parents would help them. They said they'd gotten themselves into the mess, so they could just get themselves out. And, of course, they didn't know anything about the Lord, so they didn't have anyone to help them outside themselves. I'm not saying everything is easy if a person is a Christian. But at least we know God is there."

"You said 'we' a few minutes ago. Do you have other brothers and sisters besides Ruth?"

She saw the muscles in his jawline tighten, and then he nodded. "One brother."

The hurt and anger in his voice was stark and kept her from asking questions. She reached to hold his hand and listened as he said, "Rick is four years older than I am. He was really hurt, really scarred by what happened. He was enough older that he had this sense of desertion a lot stronger than I did. When you're two, if you have enough to eat and a

74

good bed to sleep in and kids to play with, it isn't so bad at first—if you've got a teddy bear to take to bed to be with you in the dark."

Peggy swallowed tears as she heard his attempt at a laugh. "Where is Rick? Does he live at home?"

He threw his hands wide. "We don't know where he is. He got into drugs in this little town where we lived and finally dropped out of school in his junior year. No point in his going anyway if he just sat there in a daze, not knowing what was going on. Then he pulled out. Now, I guess, he just drifts."

"You never hear from him?"

He shook his head. "Every time my mother reads in the paper about someone in his twenties whose body is found somewhere along the road, she thinks—she thinks—" After a moment he went on, "And, of course, she blames herself. She can't ever forget that some part of her is out there somewhere, maybe cold and hungry and—and lost because of her selfish actions when she was young. And my dad's, too, of course."

Peggy waited until she could control her shaking voice and then said, "It's funny the way I've been envying you. I thought you must always have had an easy life. You seem so—so confident, so sure of what to do and what to believe."

"I learned to be self-reliant pretty young. Probably all kids in orphanages do."

"But you had your brother there to depend on."

He shook his head. "He wouldn't let me count on him to help. If some kids took one of my toys, he made me get it back. If I got knocked down, I had to get up by myself. He told me I had to learn not to trust anyone. But I didn't want to learn that. I wanted someone I could trust. I guess I wanted the security of love. When I found that is one of the things God offers in salvation, I really went for it. Those verses like, 'I will never leave you nor forsake you,' and the one in Psalm 27:10, 'When my mother and my father forsake me, then the Lord will take care of me,' really mean a lot to me."

Peggy finally broke the silence that fell between them. "It's funny how you think you know a person when you don't really, because you don't know all that's made him the way he is. Maybe we wouldn't be so critical of people if we tried to understand them. We look at the outside and don't try to see what the inside is like."

She felt like a hypocrite even saying the words when she knew how much she was doing that with Phyllis. She heard John almost echo her thought when he said, "I need that reminder every time I look at Dan. Now there's a guy who needs shaking up. He needs a punch in the nose."

"John!"

"Speaking figuratively, that is." Then he looked at her. "You still don't see it, do you?"

"See what? No. Dan is—Dan. He's the way he is because he's had a hard—l-ife—" She let the words trail off. How could she say that now to John?

She suddenly realized that she was cold and stiff from sitting so long in one position. "I guess I'd better go in. It's kind of late, and I'm supposed to be bright and shiny for the little kids in Sunday school tomorrow."

He reached a hand to pull her up, opened the storm door, and waited while she unlocked the door. "Thanks for listening, Peggy. You're the only one I've ever told this to. You are a very special person." He smiled down at her and then put his arms around her in a quick hug.

"Thanks," she whispered. She pushed the door open and slipped through, closing it quietly. She listened to his car as he backed out of the driveway and couldn't keep back the fervent, "Thank You, God!"

# 9

That glimpse into John's past made Peggy look at the kids around her in a way she never had before. Because she loved school, she had never thought much about the ones who didn't and who struggled every day to make it through. Some, like Alice and Ellen, really worked and wanted to pass. But she began to think of others she passed in the halls and sat with in class who never bothered to complete assignments. They seemed to just drift through each day. *Drift* was the word John had used about Rick.

She wondered how many of the kids she'd been in school with all these years were potential Ricks, and she began to study faces and watch actions. She hadn't thought about their school's having a serious drug problem until rumors went around that the police were going to bring in dogs to sniff out drugs the way it had been done in some of the big cities.

It turned out to be just a rumor, but it made Peggy aware in a new way of the levels of culture even in their fairly small school. One was their crowd who went to church from choice, had Monday morning Bible study, ate lunch together, laughed at their "in" jokes, went to school games but not the school dances, didn't know the plots of the R-rated movies, listened to gospel music tapes.

The other extreme were the kids who had so fascinated Alice once with their disdain for rules, who cut school and wrote their own excuses, sat on the edge of the schoolground with cigarettes and pot, sneered at anyone who talked about patriotism or school spirit, were into hard rock and the latest dances.

Peggy was sure that in between was a big group of kids who stood on the fringe and could be swayed one way or another. And she wondered if those in her group were just getting too satisfied with themselves.

She asked Ellen the question one day, finishing, "Sometimes I get to feeling that we're a little clique, just daring anyone to try to break through the Christian wall."

"What do you suggest we do?" Ellen asked with her usual directness.

"To start with we could break up at lunch and not eat together. And not all bunch up in the same place at games. You know we've invited a lot of kids to come to church activities—fun things, I mean, that we thought they'd like. Yet sometimes I have the feeling that it's a them-and-us deal. We don't act as though we really care about *them*. Do you see what I'm trying to say?"

"Yeah, but I'm not sure I agree all the way. No matter how interested we are in them, nothing will happen unless they are interested back. Take Phyllis, for example."

"I don't mean only those kids. I'm thinking about—well, there's a girl in my lit section. I don't know her name, even though I read one of her themes a few weeks ago. I knew when I read her paper that she doesn't know what she believes about anything. Sounded like just a—a vacuum there. So what did I do? Nothing."

John had joined them in time to hear her last few sentences, and she turned to him. "The reason I feel so bad about it is that that was the time I was

78

so proud of myself for 'sharing my testimony in class.' What good did it do her if I've never said a friendly word to her?"

"I'm willing to try," Ellen said. "Tomorrow I'll find someone I've never eaten with before and see what happens."

It worked for Ellen. She ate with a different bunch every day that week, and by Friday held up a circled thumb and first finger to Peggy from two tables away where she was obviously the life of the party.

But Peggy was discouraged. The girl in lit class was totally unresponsive to any conversation she started. She had made up her mind she was going to work on Phyllis, too, but found that Phyllis didn't eat in the cafeteria. The few times they passed in the hall, she let her eyes flick over Peggy with complete disinterest.

"She gives me the creeps," Ellen complained one day. "She just stares at you out of those funny-looking eyes with absolutely no change of expression on her face. It's like she's wearing a mask. I just wonder what she thinks about. If she thinks."

"According to Candy, she's smart. I guess she'd have to be to stay in school without studying. You know she can't be taking all Mickey Mouse courses."

"It isn't her eyes that are strange, Ellen," Alice said, her soft voice quiet. "It's all the gooky stuff she puts on them. She loads it on without being the least bit subtle about it. I guess nobody ever told her that a little bit is good, but a lot isn't."

"Who's going to be the one to tell her? Let her mother do it. Mine would," Ellen retorted.

"I guess that's part of the trouble," Peggy said soberly. "Her mother, that is. From what Candy says, Phyllis's mother pretty much ignores her. She's always out somewhere."

"Well, my mother doesn't exactly wait at the door with open arms when I come home," Ellen said impatiently. "After all, we *are* growing up."

"No, but at least you know your mother loves you. Apparently her mother makes it very clear that she is a nuisance and in the way and that she'll be glad when she's gone."

"Oh. Sorry." Ellen frowned, drumming her fingers on the table. "Well, I'd sure do something for her if I knew what, but I never see her anyway. It would have to be someone she'd listen to—preferably a boy." Then she grinned and added quickly, "Meow!"

When John met Peggy at the locker after school, he said, "I want you to promise you won't mention Phyllis's name once while I'm walking you to work. Promise?"

"Sure, but why?"

"Because I want to talk about us for a change and hold hands and talk nonsense and tell you what a special person you are and let you tell me that." His eyes had warm lights in them as he smiled down at her, tucked her arm in his, and walked her briskly out of the building and along the street. He left her laughing at the entrance to the store, the cold air and his jokes lifting the tension she had felt all day.

She had worked about a half hour when she saw Candy come in and wave at her. When there was a break at her counter, Candy come over with a can of hair spray.

"Hi. Is it against the rules to talk?"

"Not when someone is buying out the store the way you are." Peggy rang up the money, gave change, and then asked, "Or is your purchase just an excuse to talk?"

"Just an excuse, I guess," she said and then stood folding the sales slip in narrow lines, her head bent as though she had to focus carefully on the movement of her fingers.

Trying to give her an opening, Peggy asked, her voice light and free after the fun conversation with John, "What's doing with you?"

"You mean Bill doesn't keep you posted?"

"I hardly see him these days. He comes staggering in late for dinner as though the future of the basketball team rested on his shoulders, and actually he's not even a starter. And of course the quartet practices like crazy a couple of nights a week. Or, at least, three of them do. By the way, what's the matter with Dan? Do you know?"

Candy shook her head. "No, what?"

Peggy looked at her, puzzled. She didn't seem to be on track somehow. There surely couldn't be anything wrong between her and Bill. "I thought maybe Bill had said something to you about Dan. He hasn't been showing up to practice, and it kind of throws the other guys off. John told me that much is how I know, because Bill hasn't said much about it."

"I guess Bill is—pretty—busy." Both the words and the tone of voice sounded so forlorn that Peggy looked at her in surprise. "What do you mean, you guess? Don't you know? Don't you see him?"

"Yes, of course," she answered quickly. "But you know my mother doesn't let me date on school nights. And he's busy anyway with basketball and—and everything else." She waited a moment, still intently studying the sales slip, and then said, "He really means it when he says he wants to get new kids into the church group, doesn't he?"

"I think he's been too busy to do much of that. Or at least he's not spreading himself so thin the way he was doing. For a while there he said he was going to invite a different person every day. But lately he's been concentrating on just a few at a time. He is still working on Phyllis and the other two."

"He doesn't—say—anything about her?"

"You mean, whether she's going to come to anything? No, I don't think he's had much luck."

"No, I mean, just—just around the house, sort of."

Peggy frowned as she looked at Candy, who stood leaning against the counter, her head turned away. Suddenly she realized what Candy was getting at and exploded, "If you mean does he talk about her like he likes her, of course not! Are you crazy?"

She looked at her watch. "Wait a minute. I'm through in just a couple of minutes. I've got to check my drawer in, and we can talk on the way home."

Candy held the door as they pushed through and said, "I was sure he didn't. But some of the kids around school who see them in class said he—he did. And that she likes him."

"Well, I'm sure she does! But what makes them think that he likes her?"

"I don't know. I guess they've seen him talking to her in the halls—"

"Is there any crime in that? You know how friendly Bill is. He'd invite—good night—he'd invite *anybody* to church. Why don't you talk to him between classes and shut those gossipers up?"

"Our schedules are completely different this year. We don't have any classes or even lunch together. I guess that's why some kids think we've broken up. And anyway, he could date someone else. We aren't going steady."

"Oh, no! Not my darling brother! He might let a girl know he likes her and get her time all sewed up, and then say he doesn't believe in going steady."

"I think he's right," Candy said firmly. "I agree we're too young to go steady. I don't mind that part. We could break up. It's just—I couldn't stand it if he ditched me for someone like Phyllis."

"Don't be silly!" Peggy scoffed. "You should know Bill better than that by now."

"You won't tell him I asked about it, will you? I mean, if he *should* like her, I guess that's his business. And if he doesn't, I don't want him to know I thought he did."

"I won't tell him," Peggy promised, but she made up her mind to give him some helpful, sisterly advice as fast as possible.

She had intended to wait until the right time and place and be very tactful in the way she went about it. Then Ellen called that evening and sharpened the urgency when she asked, "What is this with Bill and the green-eyed monster?"

"What do you mean?"

"I heard today he was going with her, really going, I mean. I couldn't believe it."

"Well, don't, because he isn't!" Peggy retorted. "My brother might not be very bright in some things, but I know he's smart enough not to do that."

Then she added in a calmer voice, "Really, Ellen, knowing Bill, I'm sure he's just being nice to her. Haven't you been ashamed listening to him that you can't talk about the Lord as easily as he does? I have, and I don't mind admitting it, even if he is my brother."

"So you're saying someone's imagination is working overtime, huh?"

"Yes, and maybe it's Phyllis herself who is spreading the rumors. Except I don't see why she would want to date him. They are poles apart in every way. You know he wouldn't cover up his faith. It's too much a part of him."

"Maybe he'd better stop being so nice to her," Ellen suggested.

"Maybe I'd better give him some advice."

She decided to forego any preliminaries and wade right into the subject that evening while their parents were out. There was no point in getting them worked up over something they wouldn't understand. *Especially Mother*, she thought.

Unconsciously she repeated Ellen's words as she stood in the open door of his room and asked, "Hey, what is this with you and Phyllis?"

She hadn't known what kind of reaction to expect and was totally unprepared to have him swing around to face her. His voice was desperate as he looked up at her from his desk. "Peg, what'll I *do*?" in such a pleading voice that Peggy had her answer. She knew the rumors were wrong.

"What's it all about? How did the idea get started in the first place?"

Bill ran his hand through his hair, and Peggy could see how shaken he was as he answered, "I wish I knew! I'd never even spoken to her, never paid much attention to her because—well, just because. Then I asked her to come to that picnic last month, or whenever it was. And I just did that because Candy asked me to, and that was because whoever was supposed to didn't. Whoever that was sure got me in an awful mess."

Peggy moved to sit down on the edge of the bed, guilt accusing her. But she couldn't admit that she was the one. Not now, anyway.

Bill was still talking. "And even then I didn't make it a personal invitation like—you know—just the two of us. Roy and Mike were there, too, and I just said if they weren't doing anything, they could come along. I meant all of them, you know. And they did. Then later Candy told me what kind of a home life Phyllis has, and what her mother is like, and I felt sorry for her. Anybody would—you would. It's a mess. No father and—and—other men there."

He shook his head, embarrassed. "And I thought that, after all, the Lord had saved Bob when no one thought it could happen. And I knew it wasn't an impossible idea to think that Phyllis could be, too."

"So?"

"So, since then, whenever I saw her, I'd say hi and maybe talk a few minutes just to be friendly— the way I'd be to anyone. And I always invited her to church. She's never come, of course, but I always thought that maybe the next time I invited her she would. I sure never asked her for a date!"

"But that's what kids think?"

"I don't know about anybody else, but that's what *she* thinks. That I like her. That I want to go out with her."

Peggy decided not to tell him how many other kids thought so, too, or let him know that Candy was worried and hurt. There was no point in making him feel worse than he already did. Instead she asked, "How do you know she does?"

"Well—" again he ran his hand through his hair "—well, because—"

Peggy had intended to tease him about being so conceited that he thought every girl was crazy about him. But he was obviously worried about the whole thing and looked at her anxiously.

"What can I do?" he begged.

"Just ignore her. Look the other way whenever you see her. You don't sit near her in any class, do you?"

He shook his head, and there was a note of desperate hope in his voice as he asked, "Do you think that will work?"

"Well, what can she do?" Peggy asked practically. "If you go on being friendly, naturally she'll think there's hope. But if you cut her, she'll give up on you." She stopped and looked at him, shaking her head. "I still say I would never have thought she would fall for someone like you."

She knew ordinarily that would have brought an indignant reply from him. But all he said was, "If I ever get out of this mess, I'll never get into another. Girls! They're always expecting a guy to get serious about them. Why can't they just be friendly instead of getting so personal?"

"Are you forgetting that I'm one of the 'they's' you're talking about? And that you just asked me for advice?"

"Well, do you expect John to spend every minute with you and never think about anything else?" he demanded. Then, not waiting for an answer, he went on, "Candy is sensible about it, I'm glad to say."

"She has to be," Peggy retorted. "You don't leave her any choice."

But Bill was still frowning over his problem and ignored the remark as he said, "You know this leaves it up to you girls, then."

"What?"

"Keeping things going with Phyllis. I know she has only come once, and maybe there's no chance that she ever will again. But now that we've started working on her, somebody has to keep it up."

"Maybe Candy can take over."

"Phyllis doesn't like Candy, and if I drop her she'll probably blame Candy."

"Yeah, you're right. But she's so hard to get through to. It's like she shuts off part of herself the way Mrs. Anderson says her father turns off his hearing aid to shut out what he doesn't want to hear."

"Just don't give up on her yet," Bill begged. "Maybe John would ask her—"

"Oh, no, you don't! Don't try to shove your problem onto him and get him in a mess. I'll try to take over. I know Alice will talk to her, too, although she doesn't see Phyllis any oftener than I do. The trouble is, we're all so busy."

She went to her room and spread her books out, but sat tapping her pencil on the desk. She had told Bill it was his problem, and it was. But only because she had put it there through her neglect. She read the assigned lit chapter and then had to go back and read it over again to have it make sense.

Then she heard Bill's voice, troubled and uncertain, and turned to see him standing just inside the door, his Bible in his hand.

"I have to ask you something. I've got this assignment I'm doing for Sunday school, and there's a verse here that kind of hit me. Because of what we were just talking about. It's the one where God told the prophet Ezekiel that he was responsible to tell people that they had to repent. And if he didn't, God would hold him responsible for the fact that they were lost."

He looked across the room at her as he said slowly, "I just want to be sure I'm doing the right thing by avoiding Phyllis. If I do, the rest of you have *got* to try to reach her."

# 10

Peggy went to bed that night, sobered by Bill's sensitivity. She had promised him—and God as well—that she would try to reach Phyllis. But although it was easy to make the promise, carrying it out proved difficult. For one thing, their paths seldom crossed. And when they did, Phyllis was usually with her two shadows, who always mocked her by repeating everything she said in sing-song voices.

Once Phyllis, when alone, listened to her halting words, and then asked, her eyes steady and unblinking, "How come Bill doesn't talk to me anymore when he sees me?"

Peggy hadn't expected such a direct question and stumbled over words about his being busy and having so many people to talk to. Phyllis had turned in the middle of her explanation and walked off. Watching her slouch away, her hair a frizzled orange mop this time, Peggy had called after her, "Phyllis! Wait!"

But she hadn't, and Peggy felt relieved. She couldn't explain the absurd feeling of pity that had stirred in her as she watched the slender figure push through the crowd, alone, even with people milling around her.

As the days piled up, she began to feel the pressure of having too much to do. Other activities ate up any free time she had left over from homework, church, and working at the store. One was an essay contest, sponsored for the high schools in the city by a local civic organization. The first prize for the winner in each school was a $250 scholarship toward college.

Thinking of all the school expenses looming ahead, Peggy decided to enter, even though she didn't think she had the ghost of a chance of winning. But she found the biggest problem was trying to decide what to write on from the list of suggested topics.

"If you were on a committee to choose the best essay, what subject would appeal to you the most?" she asked her father one evening. "Would you go for, 'Liberty—A Priceless Gift,' or 'Our Heritage of Freedom'? Wait a minute. How about, 'How I Can Preserve Our Liberty'?"

"I'm glad I'm not on the committee," he retorted. "But if I were, I hope I would judge on the merits of the individual essay rather than on the subject. They're all important topics."

"Sure, but they're all so hard to write on!" Peggy moaned. "Besides, fifteen hundred words are an awful lot to have to say on a subject that everyone knows about and believes in anyway. And you really have to *say* something. Mr. Doty warned us. You can't pad it."

She sighed and let her shoulders slump. "I'm sorry now that I signed up to do it. All I could think about was the money instead of the hard work involved. I don't know what makes me think I stand a change of winning anyhow."

"Can't you back out?"

She shook her head. "Oh, I suppose I could. Nobody could force me to write it. But Mr. Doty is sponsoring it in our school, and he had a terrible time drumming up enough people. He said our school only had five entries, which was the lowest and poorest showing of any school in the city."

"Who are the others?"

"We don't know. Everything is secret to give those who enter an equal chance. If I could just work up some enthusiasm for the *subject*, maybe I could get started."

She studied the list of topics again and became aware that Bill was prowling the house from the front door to the phone, to the kitchen for a sandwich and glass of milk, and back again.

"Honestly, how can a person think with you rattling around the house? Can't you sit down or go someplace?" she asked crossly.

"Look, I live here too," he retorted.

She looked at him suspiciously, caught by some excitement in his voice. "How come you're home so early, anyway? Isn't this one of the practice nights? John said he wouldn't be able to call until later."

Before he could answer the phone rang, and he snatched it up and said, "Yes?"

As he listened, a big grin spread across his face. Peggy watched him curiously, listening to the brief answers he gave. "What was that all about?" she asked when he put down the phone.

"Oh, nothing. You'll find out tomorrow." All he would say the rest of the evening to her persistent questions was, "Wait until tomorrow." Even John, when he called, only said, "If Bill won't tell you, I can't."

Her curiosity was satisfied the next day in assembly when Bill's name was announced as a nominee for president of the junior class. His friends began a feverish round of campaigning for him during the four days in the middle of November that were given to the elections. Peggy helped by doing a couple of big posters that pushed his slate of officers and by listening critically every evening to the speeches he worked out.

He put in a lot of hard work on his campaign, feeling a responsibility to win if possible, though he didn't think his chances were all that good. Peggy kept trying to reassure him, though she knew he was running against one of the best athletes in the school. But even she wasn't prepared for the landslide that swept him into office, though a couple of those who were running with him didn't make it.

A gang of kids stopped for sodas after school to celebrate his victory. "And it wasn't just the church kids who voted for him," Candy bubbled. "The principal even said it was the biggest margin he has seen in the time he's been here."

"Of course Bill is OK, but he's my brother, and I just can't get used to the idea that he's so popular."

"You'll just have to face it, Peggy. He is. Practically everybody in the junior class voted for him. I felt kind of sorry for Steve, because he really is a nice guy."

"Yeah, but what can you expect when you're running against someone who's smart and friendly and good-looking and—?"

"*Bill?*" The incredulity in her voice stood out like exclamation points, causing a roar of laughter which even Bill joined.

"You see why I don't have a chance to get conceited," he said, looking around the tables with a grin.

But John, sitting next to Peggy, said in a low voice, "He takes after you."

She glanced up at him quickly, smiling back at the teasing expression in his eyes. But she saw, too, the admiring warmth that didn't match the offhand way he had spoken, and she felt a warm glow. It was so wonderful to be part of a group and yet be liked by someone special.

Looking past Ellen sitting across from her, she could see herself framed in the mirror. She saw just her same ordinary face with the smooth, simple, shoulder-length hair and bangs that she had finally decided did the most for her. A smile lifted the corners of her mouth as she saw her reflection. How much she had mourned her appearance through the years. And now, not being beautiful like Alice didn't seem important any more.

Knowing John liked *her*, and not Alice or one of the other girls she knew were prettier and had more sparkling personalities, gave her confidence and security.

She let the talk and laughter flow around her as she remembered something she had said to John soon after she started going with him. The pattern of dating was new to her, and when John said, "You know, when I looked at you across the room the night you came late to the party, I knew you were a person worth getting to know."

"Yes, but if you get close enough, you'll see all sorts of dents and nicks and scratches."

He had laughed. "Funny you should say that right now. My mother had Ruthie helping her polish the sterling silverware last night, and Ruthie got all upset over some tiny scratches on it. My mother told her that they only added to the beauty and the value of the silver when it was genuine because the scratches blend in and become part of the patina, I think she called it. On cheap stuff the dents and scratches stand out and look ugly."

"The moral of that is be glad you're not perfect." She had laughed but then sobered when he answered, "That's right. We've got to wait for God to do that for us. Which He will someday."

She thought of that conversation again the next morning as she walked slowly toward school, waiting for Alice and Ellen to come along. She couldn't remember when the world had looked more wonderful, even now when she huddled deeper into her coat collar against the bite of the wind. She laughed as she remembered how often she had scuffed this same way to school through red and gold and green leaves. Then, when they were withered, soggy masses cluttering the sidewalks, she had felt dismal and lonely and despondent.

The memory frightened her a little because she knew her happiness shouldn't depend on weather or circumstances or people. What if her present security changed? What if John suddenly fell for someone else as easily as he had fallen for her? Would it leave her the way she was before—unsure of herself and lonely?

Then Ellen caught up with her as she neared the school building, and up ahead John's tall figure waited for her by the front entrance. Her world settled comfortably back into place with the exciting but ordered days stretching ahead. She was Peggy Andrews, honor student, a Christian, and the girl of the neatest guy in the senior class. Life was wonderful!

Turning into the east corridor on her way up to her locker a few minutes later, she caught a glimpse of Phyllis in a skirt and blouse this time instead of faded jeans. The promise she had made to Bill rang in her ears accusingly. She hadn't done a thing about it in the last few weeks, not since the day Phyllis had asked about Bill. Except for a quick prayer for her occasionally, she hadn't thought of her since. Working, slaving over the essay, helping plan the breakfast the youth group was having Thanksgiving morning, and daydreaming about John filled her days too full for anything else.

She gave a hurried glance at her watch. "I've got a couple of minutes before class," she muttered. "Maybe I can catch up with her and at least give her a friendly smile."

Grabbing the books she needed, she slammed the locker door and twirled the combination lock. She pushed and elbowed her way through the crowded hall, trying to keep Phyllis in sight. When she got to the top of the second floor stairs, she peered over the railing and caught a glimpse of the red skirt swinging its way down to the first floor. Inching her way down, she dropped a book when someone bumped her. By the time she got it picked up and reached the first floor, Phyllis was at the end of the long hall, heading toward the gym.

*Well, that's that,* she thought. *If I go clear to the gym I'll be late to class. Besides, by the time I get there, she'll probably be in the dressing room, and I wouldn't have a chance to talk to her anyway.*

She turned with a sense of relief to dash back up the almost deserted stairway and slid into class just as the bell rang. It wasn't much, but at least she had tried. And anyway, there was always tomorrow.

But by the next day she was getting so panicky over the essay that she had no time to think of anything else. The hardest part at first had been deciding on her subject. She had gone over and over the list of topics, trying to find one she could write on convincingly. She realized more than ever how right Mr. Verbeck had been last year when he had blasted the class because they were so used to their freedom and liberty that the words didn't mean anything to them.

When she had finally decided to write on "How I Can Preserve Freedom," she didn't know what to say. After innumerable starts, all of which ended in the wastebasket, she began to despair. The deadline was only a week away.

"What'll I do?" she begged one evening at dinner.

"Outline what you want to say first," her father said.

"Dad, I can't!" she protested. "All you teachers say to outline, or brainstorm, or do chicken

94

scratches, or whatever you want to call it. But that doesn't help with the words. They still have to be written."

"Your ideas have to be organized first in order to know what to write. You've done enough themes to know that, Peggy. Once you have your outline in shape, you just have to follow it and write however many paragraphs you need to develop each point. It's that simple."

"Sure—for you teachers!" She sighed again. "But this time my trouble is that I don't even have ideas to outline. I don't know what to say, and I'm stuck with the subject because I've already turned in the title. So now what do I do?"

"I can't help you, since this is supposed to be your work. But one thing to remember is that it should be personal."

"What do you mean?"

"Look at your title. It says 'I', doesn't it?" he asked.

"Well, sure. So how does that help?"

"Don't suggest ways to preserve freedom that would require half the federal government to carry out."

Peggy frowned at him. "In other words, I'm supposed to figure out what I, as a senior in my high school, can do to keep world freedom? Yikes!"

"Yes, but remember world freedom starts with individual freedom. Talk about preserving the personal liberties you know about and leave the state and national and world ones out of it. No country is free if the people are slaves to others' wishes or to their own desires."

"Hm, yeah, I see what you mean," she said after a moment. "Thanks a lot, Dad." She smiled across the table at him. "Can I quote you on that?" She cleared her throat and deepened her voice. "In a personal interview, one of the most distinguished educators in our fair city said—" and she grinned at him.

But his advice started her thinking along an entirely different angle. Gradually the essay began to take shape, although she had to cross out lines, rearrange paragraphs, and write in words between the lines and down the margins.

She had never considered herself a writer, and the only thing that kept her going was thinking of the prize. She printed "250" in big numbers on a notecard and propped it in front of her. She hoped the essay would be worth the effort she was pouring into it.

Finally, the night before the deadline, she gave it a final typing, correcting it even then as she searched for the best words to use. Just having it done was a relief. But she knew, too, that having to struggle to put her ideas on paper had helped crystallize them in her own thinking. She was surer than she had ever been that she needed to have positive convictions on subjects and not just eddy back and forth between the opinions of others.

And she realized that she had to speak up for what she believed. A Bible verse had given unexpected help one evening after she had been chewing her pen over the essay. She had put a slip of paper to mark the place in 1 Peter 3:15, and some of the words came back repeatedly. "Always be ready to give a defense to everyone who asks you a reason for the hope that is in you." She did puzzle over the next words, "with meekness and fear," and decided that God wanted His witnesses to be both bold and tactful. She hoped she had done that in the essay.

Since she had no idea who else had entered the contest, she didn't know how strong her competition was. And she didn't know which was better, to decide she hadn't won or to hope that she had. But she couldn't keep down the quivers of anticipation when she went to assembly the day before Thanksgiving where the winner was to be announced.

The principal introduced the president of the organization that sponsored the contest. As he stepped up to the microphone, Peggy saw that he had two long envelopes in his hand. She hadn't known there was also to be a second-place winner and felt her hopes rise a little.

After thanking those who had entered the contest and cracking a couple of feeble jokes, the man became very serious.

"One of the rules governing this contest is that each essay, in order to be eligible, must be signed. We have had one essay submitted, an excellent one, but without a name. Since it is so very good, we would like to do something rather unusual and give that person the opportunity to identify himself or herself right now."

He waited out the rustle of movement as everyone turned to see if anyone was standing.

"I must tell you frankly that this essay was judged the best and would certainly win first place. However, if its authorship is not indicated, we can only award the first prize to the next best entry."

Again he waited until the principal got up and whispered to him. He nodded, but with obvious reluctance.

"It seems fitting, then, that one among you whose family originally came from a background of oppression and fear is the one to receive the top award for his essay on 'Freedom to Live.' Will Daniel Schwartz please come forward?"

Peggy couldn't believe it as she joined in the applause for Dan while he walked from his seat near the back of the auditorium up to the front and onto the platform. She hadn't dreamed that he had entered and was glad for his parents' sake that he had

97

won. She didn't think the applause was as enthusiastic as it ought to have been, though she clapped hard.

She heard the whisper behind her. "He probably expected to win. He's the most conceited person I've ever seen. I didn't even clap for him, and I hope he knows it."

Peggy wanted to turn around and say, "He isn't conceited, really. That's just a shield he pulls around him for protection. Inside he's scared stiff he'll be laughed at." But she didn't.

Instead she turned her attention to the platform and caught the tail end of what the man said. "—so easy these days to pass the responsibility to someone else. This essay points out that every individual, and particularly every young person today, must know what he himself believes in order to shape the opinions of others and the destiny of his world."

Listening, Peggy wondered what Mr. Doty was thinking about the unnecessary words the man was using and was sure he was mentally scratching out some of them. Then she heard, "The second prize of one hundred dollars is awarded to Margaret Andrews."

She was so unused to hearing her real name that it took a nudge from the person next to her to get her on her feet. The applause followed her to the platform and back down again, and she was glad she didn't have to walk as far as Dan had.

As soon as assembly was over, she tore open the envelope and looked at the check and the citation that was part of the award. Even a hundred dollars was something!

"Pretty neat!" Ellen exclaimed, leaning over a couple of rows of seats.

"I didn't see how you could help but win," John said admiringly, and Peggy smiled at him, grateful for his confidence.

"I almost told everyone you'd entered, I was so sure you would win," Bill said. "I'm just sorry it was the second place."

"It's really third," Peggy reminded him. "And actually, I wouldn't have won at all if the one who wrote the anonymous essay had admitted it."

"Sure wonder who it was." Then Bill looked beyond Peggy, and she turned to see Mr. Doty motioning to her. She went over to where he stood with Dan and the three others who had entered the contest.

"Do any of you have any idea who else planned to enter the contest? I know those entering were not to tell anyone else. But if you know—?"

He looked from one to the other and watched them shake their heads. He pursed his lips and tapped a long, thick envelope on the back of one of the seats. Then he abruptly dismissed the other three and said, "Peggy and Dan, come along to the office for a few minutes. We have a photographer here to take your picture."

They followed him silently, Peggy wishing she could duck into the washroom long enough to run a comb through her hair. As though reading her thoughts, the photographer smiled at her. "I've got to get all the dope on names for the story. I haven't seen a girl yet who can have her picture taken without getting a chance to look at her face." He looked at Dan. "Or a boy either, for that matter. Go ahead, while I get lined up here."

The photographer took a half dozen shots with so many wisecracks that Peggy and Dan couldn't help laughing at him. Mr. Doty stopped them before they left the office.

"I'm not at liberty to say too much about this situation, and I want you both to keep what I say in strictest confidence. We are most anxious to know who wrote the anonymous essay. If it was written seriously, we feel the person is very much in need of help. It reads very much like one that was written last year, but we know who that person is. I am telling you two this so that if you hear anything at all, *any* clue as to who the person is, you can pass the information on either to the principal or to me."

They nodded back at him, impressed by the seriousness of his manner. As they left the office, Peggy smiled at Dan. "I'm sorry for whoever the person is. But it's a good thing for me they don't know, or I wouldn't have won anything. In case I get puffed up, I have to remember that I *really* only got third place." She laughed. "I expect, though, that after a while Bill will remind me of that."

She half-expected him to say something about his prize really being second place. Instead he shrugged, his head up and his voice stiff. "I consider that I won the first award. The other one only seems so great because there is some mystery connected with it."

He turned abruptly and walked off, leaving Peggy staring after him, her mouth open in surprise and anger. "Well, of all the nerve!" she sputtered.

Then aware that she was already late for class even though Mr. Doty had given her a pass, she dashed upstairs. *I'm glad I didn't defend him after all to whoever it was who called him conceited,* she fumed inwardly. He *was* conceited and certainly had no reason to be. Writing one little essay and getting a prize had really gone to his head.

# 11

She didn't have time to fume over Dan very long, because the rest of the day went by in a whirl of activity. Ordinarily the day before a holiday dragged, with everyone watching the clock. But this one didn't. It was exciting to win something, even if it was only a second—or third—place. She found herself bubbling as she showed the award at the lunch table.

"I only hope one of you isn't the anonymous author," she said and laughed as she looked around the table. "I'd feel kind of silly showing this third place off if I thought someone here was really the writer in the group."

But in the general laughter, she remembered the seriousness of Mr. Doty's voice, almost the worry in it, and it bothered her. Surely none of her friends was in need of help. *Phyllis?* Ridiculous! She needed help, certainly, but she wouldn't bother entering a school essay contest.

She listened then as Ellen said, "Don't look at me. I can't even make out a grocery list for the things we need tonight, so how could I write on some high-toned subject?"

"What are you buying?" Alice asked and then answered quickly, "Oh, I forgot. You're getting the flour and stuff for the cinnamon rolls. I guess I just thought Mrs. Springer was buying it all."

"We didn't want her to because we were afraid she'd insist on paying for it. Especially since we'll be messing up her kitchen making the rolls and stashing them in her freezer." Ellen hauled out her list as she answered.

"What time are we supposed to be there?"

"As soon after supper as you can make it," Peggy replied. "My mother says the recipe is real easy, but of course she's done it hundreds of times and not for as many people. But we'll have a bunch helping if everyone comes, so it shouldn't take us too long."

Of the eight girls who had promised to help, only five showed up at the Springers' that evening. "Oh, well, if any more came, we'd only get in each other's way," Lois said.

"Probably," Ellen agreed. "But I thought Candy was coming. I almost called to ask if I could pick her up, but I thought Bill would probably walk her over. Since it's the night before a holiday, I thought her mother would relent on the ban against the in-the-week dating."

"I don't think he planned to," Peggy answered. "He said at supper that the quartet was going to practice tonight. Or at least that part of it was," she added hastily with a sidelong glance at Alice.

Bill had also made some digusted remark about Dan's being too busy again tonight.

"I know he's not doing anything with Alice because she's helping make rolls, and then she's sleeping over here tonight," she had told Bill, and he had frowned. "I wonder what he's doing then?"

She listened as Alice said, "Dan told me this afternoon that he wouldn't be able to play in the service tomorrow, so I guess he thought there was no use practicing."

"Speaking of Dan," Ellen exclaimed. "I never knew he had so much talent. Did any of you?"

Peggy knew she didn't really want to join in praising Dan after what he had said yesterday, but she was sure Ellen would notice and ask questions. So she asked, "Did you know he was writing for the contest, Alice?"

She nodded, her shimmering hair falling forward slightly to hide her face. "He mentioned he might."

She was apparently absorbed in measuring out the required amounts of sugar and cinnamon. Knowing her so well, Peggy was sure she wouldn't say anything more, her sense of loyalty keeping her from criticizing him. Peggy admired the quality but found it exasperating, especially now when it concerned Dan.

Thinking of his attitude that afternoon, other things she had noticed about him pushed their way into her consciousness. She remembered John's surprise at seeing Dan the night he came to the party and finding that he was a Christian.

"Arrogant" was the word John had used about him once. Peggy remembered now how she had challenged him. "You don't know Dan very well if you think that," she had said.

He had looked at her searchingly for a moment but had made no further comment. And now Peggy wondered and looked at Alice with a vague sense of unease. Perhaps her assessment of Dan was wrong, even though she had known him for so many years, and John's snap judgment was right.

"Hey, cut it out!" she hollered and ducked away from Ellen, who grinned at her and tried to hide the ice cube she was shifting from one hand to the other.

"What's the big idea?" she demanded and rubbed the back of her neck. "That was cold."

"We've been trying to get your attention for the last ten minutes, and all you do is stand there mooning around over that recipe. What's it got on it—a note from John?"

103

"Very funny!"

"Well, something sure had your attention. We've been wondering how many to expect for breakfast. Got any idea?"

"No, but—"

"We really should have had the kids sign up in advance," Alice interrupted. "Then we would have known how many rolls to make. This way we'll either have too many or not enough."

"With Bill and Jim—and Tom—there you couldn't *possibly* have too many," Peggy insisted. "You should see how many Bill eats at home. Anyway, my mother figured out the proportions on the basis of thirty kids. She didn't think more than that would drag themselves out early on a holiday, and maybe she's right. She told me this much dough will make a hundred rolls. And we can make them smaller if we have to."

Ellen put her hands on her hips and looked around at the pans lined up all over the counters and the wide table and said, "If you ask me, I think we're crazy to do all this work. We could just have bought rolls and have done with it."

"You're so right," Peggy agreed. "Whose goofy idea was this anyway?"

"Yours," Alice answered calmly. "When we first talked about fixing a Thanksgiving breakfast, someone said why not have scrambled eggs and cinnamon rolls. You chimed in and said your mother had a great recipe and why didn't we do them ourselves. So here we are," and she held up her hands, sticky with dough.

"Next time clamp your hand over my mouth if I look as though I'm going to come out with another neat idea like this," Peggy begged her.

"This is one time we'll have to hope nobody brings anyone extra so we'll have enough to go around," Lois said as she slid a couple of pans into the oven.

"Don't let them bake too long," Peggy cautioned. "If we do, they'll be too hard when they are reheated in the morning."

"If any extras come, we'll each have to eat just one apiece," Alice said, answering Lois's worry. "With Mrs. Springer scrambling the eggs, there will be plenty of them at least."

"I still wonder what happened to Candy," Ellen broke in. "She doesn't usually say she'll do something and then not show up. Not that we need her to help, but I just think it's funny. You're sure she didn't go someplace with Bill?"

"No, I'm not sure. All I know is Bill said he was going to practice all evening and he wouldn't do that by himself without at least some of the other guys. Why not call her if you're so worried?"

"Good idea. And since you suggested it, go ahead." Ellen picked up the kitchen extension and handed it to her.

Peggy made a face at Ellen and dialed Candy's number. She let it ring a long time before reluctantly putting down the receiver. "Guess she's not home. Bill must have changed his mind—or got through early and took her out for pizza."

"While you're on the phone, why not call Phyllis and tell her about the breakfast tomorrow?" Alice suggested, her voice hesitant.

Ellen shook her head. "It would just be a waste of time," she said impatiently. "Besides, we've just been talking about not having enough. If she came she'd bring the other creeps—" She stopped, bit her lip, and mumbled, "Sorry."

"She won't come," Peggy said. Then the memory of Bill came back as he had stood in her room with his Bible, talking about Ezekiel and asking her to please see that someone looked after Phyllis.

She turned with a sigh and looked up the number. She listened to the phone ring a half dozen times before she put it down and turned, trying not to show her relief. There would be another chance to ask her to something that would be more appealing to her.

Mrs. Springer came into the kitchen, sniffing the fragrance of the baking rolls. "If those taste as good as they smell right now, you won't have any trouble getting rid of them. I've had to chain my boys to their beds to keep them from coming down for a handout."

"If they were older, we'd let them come, even if there weren't any left for tomorrow's breakfast," Shirley said so emphatically that they all laughed.

"Right now girls are out in left field as far as they are concerned. Except for Ellen, that is," and Mrs. Springer smiled across the room at her.

"It's nice to know *some* boy is crazy about me, in this case two of them, even if they are ten years younger than me." Ellen took a big bite of the pie Mrs. Springer had cut and passed around.

Peggy happened to look up and caught the thoughtful, compassionate expression on Mrs. Springer's face as she looked at Ellen for a moment. And Peggy's memory flashed back to the scene in the store at Bill's victory celebration. She and John had been smiling at each other, and she had looked at herself in the mirror, flushed with happiness. Her eyes had slid over Ellen at the time, but now her memory saw the wistfulness on her face as she had sat, the odd person at a tableful of couples. *The way I used to be,* she thought, and she felt her throat constrict in sympathy for Ellen.

Then Shirley said, "I just love to come to your house, Mrs. Springer. Everything is so restful."

Even Mrs. Springer joined in the shout of laughter, and she exclaimed, "I think that's the nicest compliment I've ever had. My house and everyone in it have been called loud, splashy, colorful, too gaudy, 'with it,'—whatever that means—but never restful."

"I guess that's the wrong word. I mean—secure—confident—at ease. That's how I meant it. My dad used to be in the service, and when he says, 'Attention!' we know we're in for it. When he says, 'At ease,' we can relax."

"I go along with Shirl on that," Ellen said. "When I come over with a question, I know I can relax because I'll get an honest answer. You don't pretend. Maybe I won't like the answer, but at least I know you'll tell me things straight."

"I've found out something more important than that." Lois's usually shy voice was so positive that they all looked at her. "I've discovered that there are families that are whole, like this one. I guess you don't know that I live with my grandparents because my parents split up and neither of them wanted me. I never wanted anyone to know that because I was ashamed. Then I started finding out that lots of other kids had split families, not just in school but in church, too. Like you, Ellen, and you, Shirl. And I decided I never was going to get married if that's the way marriage turned out. But now I know it doesn't have to."

"Lois has hit on something very important," Mrs. Springer said into the silence. "Some of you are dating, and some of you aren't. I just want to say to all of you to be careful whom you date. Get to know him well—his interests, his goals, his dreams, the way he treats his mother or sisters." She smiled faintly at that, but it didn't take away the earnestness of her voice. "Be honest with one another, and don't play games with one another's emotions. And be sure the one you date is a Christian."

"You mean, we shouldn't go out with anyone who is not a believer?" Shirley's voice was questioning.

"In a group as a casual fun gathering, perhaps. In single dating, no."

"But you might help that person come to know the Lord."

Peggy caught the troubled sound in Alice's voice and listened as Mrs. Springer answered carefully, "You can't carry fire in your hand without getting burned. And our emotions can be like fire, burning faster than we can control them. The first time you date someone, let him know where you stand in your relationship to the Lord. If he doesn't want any part of it, he will drop you. And I know sometimes that's hard to take. Sometimes girls grab for happiness and find it turns to ashes. Always wait for God to show you what He wants for you."

"What if—if that means you never get married?" Shirley's voice was muffled.

"I can only say that if that is what God has planned for you and you accept it, God gives other kinds of happiness." She looked around at their faces under the bright kitchen lights and moved briskly. "Save your questions, and we'll have some more sessions. Right now, there are only a few hours until we'll be watching all your hard work disappear into hungry stomachs."

Peggy didn't realize until she and Alice were ready for bed that Alice had been unusually quiet all evening. "Is everything OK?"

"What Mrs. Springer said really made me think. About Dan, I mean."

"I don't get the connection exactly."

"He's been so different lately, and I've wanted to say something to him, but he never gives me a chance."

"Different? How?"

"You know how moody he's always been. Underneath he's nice and likeable, if you can stand being around him long enough to find that out. It was sort of like he wore a mask of hardness and conceit to cover up the way he really felt inside. I've always thought he didn't want anyone to know that he was pretty tenderhearted. But lately it seems as though the mask has become his real self. He really thinks he is the most important person around. Like this contest. He really expected to win."

"Yeah, he told me that this morning and acted as though there shouldn't have been a second-place winner because it took some of the glory from him."

"Well, a person shouldn't be like that, should he?" And Alice added a troubled, "If he is a Christian."

Peggy caught the drift of the conversation and saw the connection with what Mrs. Springer had said. She thought again of John's doubts about Dan. *How does anyone know a person's heart?* she wondered. And the logical answer was, *By his actions.*

"His parents are really broken up about it," Alice went on in her sweet, troubled voice. "His mother is so naive. She doesn't even understand all his sarcastic remarks, but she hears how his voice sounds, and it hurts her."

"How long has he been like this?"

"I don't know. Maybe always, and I haven't seen it before."

"He always has been touchy about things, and we always just said, 'Oh, that's the way Dan is.' He was like that the first time I ever saw him, when he and his parents came to our house for Thanksgiving dinner—good night! Five years ago now."

"And he's so sensitive about the fact that his father is just a janitor in an office building."

"I thought he was over that by now," Peggy exclaimed impatiently. "He doesn't think people look down on him for that, does he? And besides, Mr. Schwartz himself is proud of his job. I've heard him tell lots of times how he meets so many interesting people and has a chance to witness to them. He says he likes the responsibility he has of locking up all the doctors' offices in the building and knowing he is keeping everything safe. I think it's kind of corny myself, but you can tell he means it. And, anyway, he must make pretty good money. Dan always has sharp clothes and money for things, and he doesn't even have a part-time job the way a lot of the guys do."

"But Dan doesn't see it that way. He likes to have money, sure, but *being* somebody is more important to him than anything else. I sometimes think he only wanted to go with me in the first place because Bob was," she finished miserably.

"I don't think so," Peggy said positively. "He liked you right from the start. He's always been a lone-wolf type and hard to get to know. But—" she frowned as she thought of what she wanted to say "—if you think he's just pretending to be a Christian, which I don't think is true, well—" She stopped again. "Mrs. Springer would say, 'Quit going with him.'"

She knew Alice was remembering the conversation in Mrs. Springer's kitchen, too, when she said, "The trouble is, I like him. I like him a lot. I've wanted to say something to him about the way he's been acting, but I was afraid he'd get mad and not want to go with me anymore. But now I'm wondering. Maybe I'm not being honest with him, not being really a friend as well as a girl friend. But I don't know what to say, or how."

"I see what you mean. He wouldn't like it at all if you criticized him even in a nice way and for his own good. Maybe one of the guys could. Or Mr. Parker."

"Someone ought to. It scares me, because it isn't right for a Christian to act the way he does."

Her voice ran down as she crawled into bed and snapped off the light. Peggy didn't know what to say to make her feel better. It was funny how things worked out, she thought, lying in the shelter of the dark room. For so many years she had envied Alice's ease in dating and the smooth way things worked out for her with all the guys wanting to take her out. And now it was she who had the problems.

*I hope I'll always remember this,* she thought, hanging on to the wonder of her own contentment and happiness with John. *I hope I'll always be willing to wait for God to work in just the right way and not rush in the way I think is right.*

Before she drifted off to sleep, the memory of Phyllis nibbled at her conscience. She made a firm resolution that, no matter how hard it was, or how much effort it took, or how many times Phyllis tuned her out, she was going to go all out in getting her to church. Phyllis simply *had* to find out what it meant to be a Christian.

# 12

Neither of them heard the alarm go off the next morning. It was Bill's staccato pounding on the door and his worried, "Hey, aren't you two supposed to be over at the church getting breakfast?" that brought them to a frantic awareness of how late it was.

Peggy leaped out of bed. "We won't make it! I don't feel as though I even closed my eyes all night. I hope a shower will wake me up." Then, remembering her manners, she asked, "Do you want to go first?"

"No, go ahead. I'll get my stuff in my overnight bag while you're showering. Hurry it up, though." Alice yawned, not stirring from her comfortable, curled-up position under the warm covers.

Peggy eyed her suspiciously. "Are you thinking of going back to sleep?" she demanded. "If you are—"

A car horn blasted outside the window, followed almost immediately by the sound of the doorbell. "I'll bet that's Ellen already. We're supposed to get the rolls at the Springers' on the way to church. We'd better step on it!"

She disappeared into the bathroom, hoping Alice wouldn't make them any later than they already were. When she came out to let Alice in for a shower, Ellen was standing around impatiently.

"What did you do? Talk all night?" she demanded, helping make the bed and cram Alice's things into her overnight case.

"Uh-uh, just half," Peggy retorted. "The way you and I usually do. But this is about the fastest I've ever had to dress."

When they clattered down the stairs ten minutes later, she stopped at the door to call back to Bill. "How about phoning Candy to see if she can come over and help? She wasn't supposed to have to work on this thing, but since we're getting a late start, we sure could use her. I don't think she'll mind."

"OK," Bill said and started for the phone. "It's only seven o'clock, so her mother will probably chew me out for calling so early, especially on a holiday."

Peggy dashed out to the car, which Ellen had already started. Mrs. Springer had the pans of rolls stacked and ready to go, and the others who were helping were already at the church when Ellen pulled into the parking lot. Mrs. Springer gave orders so efficiently that everything got done with a minimum of confusion in spite of their rush.

Bill came in just as Peggy was putting a glass of tomato juice at each place. His face settled into an anxious frown as he looked around the room and then glanced into the kitchen.

"Isn't Candy here?"

"No. Did she tell you she would be? As it happens we got along all right without—"

"I wonder where she can be?"

"Did you call her?"

"Yeah, and her mother answered. She said Candy wasn't there and slammed the phone down right away. Her voice sounded kind of funny, but I just figured she was mad, as usual, because Candy was coming to a church thing. And I thought maybe I woke her up. But I figured that meant Candy must be here already. Where would she be this early in the morning?" The worried look was back on his face.

But Peggy hurried back to the kitchen for more juice and said, "She probably had just left and will be here any minute."

But Candy didn't come. Peggy noticed during the breakfast that even the cinnamon rolls, which were perfect, didn't have Bill's complete attention. He even persuaded Alice to call Candy's house before the service began.

She came back, shaking her head at him. "Nobody answered."

When their father came a little later, they met him in the lobby, and Bill said, "Let's sit back here by the door for a change. OK?"

In answer to the question in her father's raised eyebrows, Peggy whispered, "Candy isn't here, and he is really shook." But she couldn't help thinking that it was odd and very unlike Candy to disappear so mysteriously.

Bill was so quiet and worried all the way home that Peggy began to feel sorry for him. When they got into the house, she took off her coat and tossed it to him. "Hang it up for me, and I'll call her."

His voice was pathetically grateful as he said, "Would you, Peg? Thanks a lot!"

He stood near her as she dialed. "If Candy answers, let me have it. If it's her mother, ask for Candy. Her mother won't know your voice, so if she says Candy isn't there, ask where she is. Her mother would tell someone else, but she sure wouldn't tell me."

Peggy nodded in response to Bill's instructions but listened to the phone ring endlessly. "It's funny how you can tell when a house is empty by the way the phone sounds when it rings," she said as she hung up.

Ordinarily Bill would have argued the point, and when he didn't, Peggy realized how worried he was. "They've probably gone someplace for dinner."

"Candy would have told me. They were going to have people in."

"Well, they must have changed their plans—"

"But why wasn't Candy home at seven o'clock in the morning?"

"Her mother was probably mad at her for wanting to go to church and just wouldn't let you talk to her. Don't get in a stew over it. Good night, you act as though she's been kidnapped or something. There's certainly some good, simple explanation."

Peggy purposely made her voice sound cross to distract Bill, but privately she thought the whole situation did seem strange.

Even the turkey and dressing and cranberry sauce didn't hold Bill's attention. When the phone rang, he jumped for it so quickly that his water glass wobbled, and only Mr. Andrews's quick movement kept it from spilling.

Peggy went to stand in the hall and saw from the relieved expression on his face that it was Candy. Then, after listening to her a moment, he said, "Sure. She's right here," and held out the phone without a word of explanation.

She took it with a curious glance at him and heard Candy's voice, tired and drained. "Peggy. I've been at the hospital all morning with Phyllis."

"With Phyllis?" Peggy heard herself repeating stupidly.

"Yes. She—she swallowed some of her mother's pills, different kinds. Quite a lot, I guess. Last night some time. They still aren't sure if she'll even live."

Her tired voice broke and stopped for a moment. Then it steadied, and Candy went on. "I'm calling to ask if you would let the Parkers know. They don't have any minister or *anybody* who knows the Lord.

Nobody has been allowed to see her yet, not even her mother because she was crying so hard and talking so loud and blaming Phyllis for doing it. I thought—if—something should happen, Mr. Parker should be here."

Candy was frankly crying, and Peggy bit her lip and heard how ragged her voice was as she asked, "How long have you been there?"

"Ever since they brought her in."

"When did it happen?"

"I don't know exactly. Sometime early this morning, I guess. Her mother woke up and saw a light on in the bathroom and Phyllis lying on the floor. She called my mother first, and we went over and called an ambulance. My mother took Phyllis's mother to our house. She sort of went to pieces. I've just been sitting here in the lobby waiting for news. I thought at least one of her friends should be here," she finished simply.

This choked Peggy more than ever as she remembered her too-late decision of last night to be nice to Phyllis. *Nice,* she thought bitterly. What a weak word for the need that Phyllis had. But she said, "I'll call Mr. Parker. I know he'll come right over."

She hung up and dialed the Parkers' number with shaking fingers. She could sense the intent, questioning silence of the family and heard her parents' murmured exclamations as she gave Mr. Parker the information.

"I'm on my way," he replied immediately and hung up.

Peggy sat down at the dinner table again but knew that none of them were hungry for the pumpkin pie and nuts her mother served for dessert.

"The poor kid!" Bill muttered once, and Peggy was sure he was thinking of Candy. Somehow there was an unreality about Phyllis, a remoteness, that

116

made it difficult to think about her with any deep emotion.

Mrs. Andrews's question, "Whatever made her do such a thing?" was the one most frequently asked the next few days. And there was no one to give an answer. Phyllis's mother remained secluded in her home, and Phyllis was isolated in the hospital. She seemed to be clinging to life but not responding to any medication or treatment.

Mr. Parker had been allowed in her room once on Saturday and had spoken to her gently for a minute. But she had lain motionless, he said, with her eyes closed, and he wasn't sure she knew that anyone was there.

He went to the hospital again Sunday afternoon and then stopped in to the meeting to give a report.

"According to the doctor, the biggest problem they face is that she doesn't seem to have a will to live. That disinterest keeps her system from responding to the treatment. If she comes through sufficiently to have a few visitors, the doctor thinks that might aid in her recovery. In the meantime, you all have the job of praying for her."

He looked around at them, his face grave. "I hope each one of you will take the responsibility seriously."

Peggy knew he wasn't directing the words at anyone in particular, but she couldn't help thinking that this was a request to her personally. If only she had *really* tried to talk to Phyllis. If only she had really *cared*. But she had been too busy with other things, things that now, in the grim light of the possibility of Phyllis's death, were so unimportant.

She knew Bill had been blaming himself ever since the news came. That afternoon, he had said, "I was so afraid of what people were thinking, that I didn't care about the effect on her if I suddenly stopped talking to her. I was only thinking of myself and my little reputation!"

117

And Peggy could only remember the question Phyllis had asked, "How come Bill doesn't talk to me anymore?" and her answer that he was busy, that he had other people to talk to. Was that what had pushed her over the edge?

As she sat through the meeting, she let her mind probe painfully back over the few short months since Phyllis had first sauntered into their consciousness. If only back then they had been alert to her. If only they had looked beyond the external shallowness to the deep inner emptiness!

Instead, they had judged her harshly, seeing only the bravado of extremes in makeup and fads. How could they—no she—have been so indifferent to her all the time they had talked so piously about "reaching out"?

The question was echoed by Ellen after the evening service, as they stood huddled in small groups on the front steps of the church.

"When I think of how I acted toward her!" she exclaimed. "I don't think I ever once said anything nice to her. I know I never thought anything nice. I was too busy gawking at the stuff on her eyes and talking about her looking like a clown. All the time I was the dumb cluck."

"I was the same way. We all were," Alice said in her soft, serious voice. "I really meant to do something especially friendly for her, and I just put it off until it was too—" She stopped abruptly.

Peggy looked at her quickly and then away, knowing she was going to say, "Until it was too late."

"But it can't be!" Candy burst out. "We've just *got* to have another chance, for our sake as well as hers."

The chance came unexpectedly late Monday afternoon. Candy called, a faint shred of hope in her voice as she said, "Peggy, would you go to the hospital tonight to see Phyllis?"

118

"Is she that much better that she can have visitors? Maybe Mr. Parker should. He would know what to say to help her."

"Her mother called my mother and said they would allow just one visitor and only for five minutes at the most. Maybe not that long even. And she wanted me to go. But I can't. I'm not sixteen yet, and they won't let me go farther than the lobby. Lots of hospitals do, but this one is stricter. And I guess it's partly because of how careful they have to be of her."

"Do you think she'd—want to—see—me?" Then, to explain her reluctance, she said, "The last time we talked just for a minute in the hall at school, I—I think I really—really hurt her, even though I didn't mean to."

"I don't know that *she* wants to see anyone at all," Candy returned soberly. "But her mother asked specially for someone from church to go. She said she didn't want anyone from the crowd Phyllis usually runs around with. So I think one of us must go."

"I think so, too. It's just that I'm scared. What if I blow it and make things worse? Maybe I could get someone to go with. Alice maybe. She's so sympathetic, and her voice is so soft and sweet."

"Her mother said she could only have one visitor. Please, Peggy! I couldn't think of anyone better to ask than you."

Peggy winced. This was like rubbing salt in an open wound. If only Candy knew what a miserable flop she had been with Phyllis.

"Oh, Peggy, wait a minute. I was going to tell you something I heard today. You know that essay contest? Well, apparently Phyllis entered it, too. Her mother was looking at things in her room, trying to find some clue to why she did this. And she found a carbon copy of an essay in her desk

119

drawer. She told my mother about it and said it was all about freedom and how she didn't have it but she was looking for it and had a plan all worked out to be free forever. It was clear, and yet it was all muddled up, too. That sure sounds as though she was the anonymous writer."

"It must be," Peggy answered, remembering Mr. Doty saying that whoever wrote it needed help desperately.

That evening as John drove her to the hospital, she made and discarded imagined conversations. "I don't know what to say to her," she said as John pulled into the parking lot. "Help me."

He reached for her hands that were clenched in her lap and gently loosened her fingers. "I'm not sure either," he said. "But I can suggest that you go in with an open heart and reaching hands and tell her that God loves her."

She nodded up at him, blinking back tears at the tenderness of his voice and the meaning of his words. He walked into the lobby with her and waited while she asked for the room number and was given a visitor's card. She took the elevator to the third floor and walked along the wide hall, looking for the number. Laughter and snatches of TV programs and music spilled out of the rooms she passed.

But Phyllis's door was closed. She knocked softly and then pushed it open. She hesitated in the doorway a moment and then walked over to the bed, struck by the fragility of the slender figure lying motionless. Phyllis's face, scrubbed clean of the layers of makeup, looked translucent in contrast to the dark eyelashes that lay against her cheeks.

As Peggy watched, Phyllis opened her eyes and stared up at her. Once again Peggy felt the intensity of the look from the dark depths as she had that day at the picnic. This time, knowing the need, she saw it. John was right in his advice.

She held out her hand. "We want you to live," she said softly. She hoped the words carried the meaning she intended them to have.

As Phyllis stared back at her, the same unfathomable look on her face, Peggy was afraid she had failed again. Then, slowly, tears welled up in Phyllis's eyes and slid silently down her colorless cheeks.

"How?" Her lips framed the question in a whisper so slight Peggy barely heard it.

It was all the invitation she needed. She sat down on the chair beside the bed and pulled from her purse a small copy of the gospel of John she had got one summer at Bible camp. She had taken it from her desk drawer at the last minute before coming over, thinking she could leave it on the table beside Phyllis's bed even if they weren't able to talk. Some of the verses were printed in heavy black type that stood out clearly on the page and could be read easily.

She held the book at an angle and followed silently as Phyllis's eyes traveled across the pages.

"For God so loved the world that He gave His only begotten Son, that whoever believes in Him should not perish but have everlasting life."

"I am the bread of life. He who comes to Me shall never hunger, and he who believes in Me shall never thirst."

"I am the resurrection and the life. He who believes in Me though he may die, he shall live."

Peggy wondered how much meaning these verses, so familiar to her, had for Phyllis who read them so intently. She had no time to comment on them because the nurse came in, put her hand on her patient's pulse, and said, "This is long enough for now."

Phyllis moved one hand slowly to lay it on the small gospel. She looked up at Peggy. "Come—back."

Her lips framed the invitation in words, but Peggy read it, too, in the mute appeal in the dark eyes. She nodded, not able to squeeze an answer through her tight throat.

She went down to the lobby and crossed to where John stood waiting for her, his eyes concerned. Once again, as so often in the past, she was conscious of a feeling of wonder at the way God worked. In spite of their failure, He was giving them another opportunity to show Phyllis His love that could fill the emptiness of her life. And for Peggy it held a special promise that her prayers for her mother, too, would be answered.

She smiled up at John through eyes still brimming with tears that had come with Phyllis's invitation.

"Everything is going to be all right," she answered his unspoken question. She walked with him through the open door into the darkness of the cold night, a darkness that was jeweled by the sparkling stars.